a girl walks
into a wedding

Also by Helena S. Paige

A Girl Walks into a Bar

a girl walks into a wedding

YOUR FANTASY, YOUR RULES

Helena S. Paige

WM

WILLIAM MORROW

An Imprint of HarperCollins*Publishers*

A GIRL WALKS INTO A WEDDING. Copyright © 2014 by Helena S. Paige. All rights reserved. Printed in the United States of America. No part of this book may be used or reproduced in any manner whatsoever without written permission except in the case of brief quotations embodied in critical articles and reviews. For information address HarperCollins Publishers, 195 Broadway, New York, New York 10007.

HarperCollins books may be purchased for educational, business, or sales promotional use. For information please e-mail the Special Markets Department at SPsales@harpercollins.com.

FIRST EDITION

Designed by Diahann Sturge

Library of Congress Cataloging-in-Publication Data has been applied for.

ISBN 978-0-06-229200-1

14 15 16 17 18   OV/RRD   10 9 8 7 6 5 4 3 2 1

How to Get the Most Fun Out of This Book

Dear Reader,

This isn't a regular novel with a set beginning, middle, and end. This is your story, and you're in charge. Of your life, your sexuality, your fantasies.

So here's how it works: At the end of every scene, you'll be given a choice, with instructions to go to the page that corresponds with your selection. It's simple: YOU pick what you want to do, where you want to go, who you want to be with. There are no right or wrong decisions. Just keep turning through the pages and you're guaranteed a wild ride that you shape and control.

Wondering "what if"? Want to try something different? Unlike in life, here you can press the reset button. Just go back to the previous fork in the road, pick something different, and head out on a new adventure.

Because remember: It's your fantasy, your rules.

Enjoy!

Helena S. Paige

 ALL WOMEN KNOW THAT bridesmaid dresses are a secret plot of the devil. No matter how much your best friend, sister, or cousin promises she will not dress you up as the Bride of Frankenstein on Disco Night, odds are you'll be walking down the aisle swathed in the kind of fabric used to upholster sofas, in the one color designed to make you look jaundiced.

But you're not feeling any bridesmaid-dress-fitting panic today. Jane is your oldest friend in the world, and you know she'd never expect you to wear a monstrosity. You've seen pictures of what she has in mind for you—a tasteful slip dress in a harmless dark-blue satin.

"Champagne?" a shop assistant asks, holding out a tray of flutes, the bubbles racing to pop out of the top of each glass.

"Yes, please," says Cee Cee, Jane's older sister and maid of honor, appearing beside you and taking one. Cee Cee adores weddings—in fact, as a wedding planner, she makes a living out of them. You're a little worried she might be infecting Jane with too much bridezilla hysteria and over-the-topness—most of the events she presides over make the royal wedding look like an elopement followed by shooters at the neighborhood dive bar—but you have to admit, she's a great organizer.

"Have you seen Jane's dress?" you ask, sinking into one of the luxurious armchairs set in front of a wall of mirrors and a little podium, designed for optimum dress viewing.

"Not yet! But I can't wait," Cee Cee says, settling down in the chair next to yours, eyes shining. "And you will just *die* when Jane tells you about my idea for the bridesmaids' dresses!"

That sounds a little alarming. You're about to ask for details, but then Jane steps out of the dressing room, closely followed by a mountain of fabric, the bridal shop owner fussing over the train of the dress.

"Oh my god, Jane!" you say.

ം If the wedding dress is magnificent, go to page 3.

ം If the wedding dress is hideous, go to page 5.

❧ The wedding dress is magnificent

 YOU CATCH YOUR BREATH. She looks stunning. The dress is white, which, as her best friend, you know is a bit of a stretch, but it's her wedding—she can have it.

It has a sweetheart neckline, a delicate lace bodice, and lace sleeves, and as she climbs onto the platform, the wall of mirrors reveals at least two dozen small silk buttons running down the length of the fitted back.

You can't believe your best friend is getting married. You were at nursery school together, you went through elementary school, then puberty, then high school together; you dated your first boys and had your first heartbreaks side by side; and now she's moving on to the next stage of her life—without you.

You're incredibly happy for her, of course, and Tom's a nice enough guy. You want to focus on her happiness, but you can't help feeling a little sorry for yourself. It's not that you're desperate to get married, it's just that you wish you didn't have this feeling she was leaving you behind.

"What do you think?" Jane asks, turning slightly to each side, showing off the full beauty of the dress.

"I'm speechless," you say.

Cee Cee is on her feet, tugging at the long, full skirt that swirls out into a train like a puddle of cream behind Jane.

"You make the most beautiful bride," Cee Cee says.

You nod, a lump in your throat.

"Okay, girls," says Jane. "Now it's your turn."

☙ To see your bridesmaid dress, go to page 12.

Helena L. Paige

❧ The wedding dress is hideous

YOU CATCH YOUR BREATH. She looks hideous.

The dress is glacier white. So white it makes your eyes ache, but it's the design that's the real problem.

The dress contains more pleats, ruffles, and shoulder pads than an entire season of *Dynasty*. The neckline plunges much too low between her breasts, and the gap is filled in with a white lace mesh. Then there are big white scrunched-up fabric flowers that look like flopped nursery-school art projects all over the bodice and the skirt, which is that awkward length, an inch too short to be long, and an inch too long to be short.

"You look absolutely stunning! That's the most beautiful dress I've ever seen!" Cee Cee gushes.

You glance at Cee Cee's face to see if she's lying, but if she is, she's masking it really well. Jane looks at you hopefully.

- To tell Jane the truth about the dress, go to page 7.

- To tell her a lie, go to page 10.

❧ You tell Jane the truth

"WELL?" JANE'S SMILE IS slipping. "What do you think?"

You seize a glass of champagne and toss it back. The bubbles make you splutter—but at least you've bought yourself some time. "I'm . . . I'm not sure white is really your color," you manage.

"White isn't a color, it's a shade," the bridal shop owner snaps, approaching with the stealth of a shark.

"So the color is the problem?" Jane says. She turns to the owner. "Do you have this in pale pink? Maybe coral?"

Pink? Coral? That would be even more horrendous. "Um . . . actually, come to think about it, it's not the color, it's the style," you say. "You've got such a great figure, Jane; I'm not sure it does you justice."

"But I've had seven sessions here. I've tried on hundreds of the damn things. Can you be more specific?"

Another gulp of champagne. "Maybe the . . . frills are a little bit over-the-top."

Jane turns to look in one of the full-length mirrors. "Do you hate it? It's important that you're honest."

"Really?"

"Absolutely. You're my oldest friend. I can take it."

Cee Cee is making throat-slitting gestures at you, and the owner and the assistant holding the tray of champagne are staring at you in undisguised horror. Everyone's waiting.

"Okay. Look, Jane, there's no nice way to say this. But . . ." You drain your glass and take a deep breath. She's your best friend, she deserves the truth. "It's hideous. It's vomitous. You look like you're wearing a couture diaper."

There's a shocked silence.

Jane glares at you. "How can you say that?"

Maybe you should have been more subtle. Blame it on the champagne. "I'm sorry. I didn't mean for it to come out like that."

"Are you jealous? Is that it? Because I've found someone I love and you haven't?"

Where did that come from? You can sense a potential doozy of a fight crackling in the air. "Jealous? No! That's not fair. You asked me for my opinion, and I gave it to you."

"Next you'll be saying that I shouldn't marry Tom!"

In fact, you're not sure that Tom, Jane's fiancé, is exactly the right guy for her, but two honesty bombshells on the same day might not be a good idea.

Tears glimmer in Jane's eyes. There's a long silence as she stares at herself in the mirror. You brace yourself for more recriminations, but suddenly she bursts out laughing. "I look like a schizophrenic Disney princess, don't I?"

"Or an explosion in a meringue factory," you add.

Jane giggles. "What was I *thinking*?"

"Well, I like it!" Cee Cee chimes in defensively, but for once Jane ignores her.

"What about something like this?" you say, going over to a rack and pulling out a sleek, vintage-style gown in ivory silk. "I saw it earlier, and I thought it would look beautiful on you."

"It is pretty," Jane says, and you and Cee Cee wait while Jane and the owner disappear behind the dressing-room curtain.

Jane reappears—and both you and Cee Cee gasp. It's gorgeous. Perfect. The deceptively simple flapper design echoes the glamour of *The Great Gatsby* era, and looks as if it was created solely to complement Jane's slim figure.

"Thanks for saving me," Jane says to you. "Okay, your turn now."

❧ To see your bridesmaid dress, go to page 12.

a girl walks into a wedding

You lie

HOW CAN YOU TELL Jane the truth? You know how many fittings she's had, the months spent poring over Vera Wang catalogs and agonizing over couture websites. Maybe the dress won't look so awful once she's had her hair and makeup done.

"It's . . . um . . . stunning," you say, your voice sounding fake even to you. You've never been a particularly good liar.

Jane frowns and takes a long look at herself in the mirror. "Really?"

"Mm-hmm." You seize a glass of champagne and take a swig.

Cee Cee nods in agreement and admiration. It's a mystery how a wedding planner can have such appalling taste.

"You don't think it's too much?" Jane asks.

"Maybe a little?" you squeak.

"I thought you said it was stunning?"

To be fair, the sight of it *would* stun anyone with taste. You bite your tongue.

"Oh god," Jane wails. "I look like a meringue wrestling a duvet." She rounds on you. "I can't believe you were going to let me wear this monstrosity!"

"Um . . . I would have told you eventually. You caught me off guard."

"What am I going to do now?"

The dress shop owner is way ahead of the game. She brandishes an elegant, vintage-looking dress with delicate embroidery. "Perhaps madam would like to try on something like this?"

Jane shoots you a dirty look and disappears behind the curtain.

But when she reappears, this time looking truly stunning, your admiration is entirely heartfelt. She twirls in front of you, and you can see from her face that all is forgiven.

"Now it's your turn," she announces.

❧ To see your bridesmaid dress, go to page 12.

a girl walks into a wedding

✎ You're seeing your bridesmaid dress for the first time

 ANOTHER SHOP ASSISTANT APPEARS with two huge dress bags and hangs them on a rack next to the fitting area.

"You're going to love this!" Cee Cee trills.

You steal another glance at the dresses in their garment bags. You strongly suspect there's a gaping chasm between what Cee Cee loves and what you love.

"I know I showed you some references before," Jane says, "and we discussed the blue satin when we did your measurements a few months ago, but when Cee Cee and I were choosing the tablecloths, we found this beautiful material that we think will complement the whole look."

"You mean our dresses are going to be made out of the same fabric as the tablecloths?" you say, trying to rein in your alarm.

"And the napkins!" Cee Cee exclaims. "Isn't it genius?

All the A-list celebs are doing it." She grabs her dress eagerly and slips into one of the dressing rooms.

Desperate not to disappoint Jane, you collect yours, smothering your sense of impending doom. Once in your stall, you hang the dress on a hook and step back to appraise it. It doesn't look promising, but maybe it won't be so bad once it's on, you think, a seed of hope still lodged in your heart.

You strip down to your undies, keeping on your Converse sneakers, then carefully step into the pile of heavy fabric. You grasp the sleeves and do battle with the dress, tugging it up over your hips and thighs. It's tight, and you have to suck in your tummy and hop up and down to get it on. At last you slip your arms into the sleeves and reach behind you to pull up the zipper, which only makes it halfway up your back before sticking. You wriggle and tug, but it doesn't budge any farther.

You hear Cee Cee squealing outside: "I told you, Jane! It's perfect!" She rips your curtain open. "How does yours look?" she asks.

You brace yourself and step out to assess the damage.

On Cee Cee, who has small, high boobs and long legs, the dress doesn't look too bad, but on you it's an unmitigated disaster. The puffed sleeves and scalloped neckline make you look like a milkmaid, and every time you breathe out, more of the little pearl buttons down the front pop open. Then there's the color. Jane promised not to make you wear any shade of sugar pink, but this—which Cee Cee insists is apricot, but

a girl walks into a wedding

looks more like stale salmon mousse—is almost worse. And—the final insult—it has a sprigged pattern. You feel like inventing a mysterious accident for it. Something involving a tsunami and a kitchen full of curry would do nicely.

The shop owner and the dressmaker descend on you. One shoves your breasts back into the cups of the dress, and the other pulls the back of the dress together and manages to get the zipper up, with the result that the remaining buttons on the bodice peel open all the way to your waist.

"It doesn't fit so well." You state the screamingly obvious.

"I'm sure they'll be able to fix it. You *will* be able to fix it, won't you?" Jane turns to the dressmaker, her voice hitting that ultrahigh frequency that only bridezillas can reach. The woman looks dubious, but then she and the owner bustle around you, pulling at the fabric and seams while you stand there, hoping that everyone attending the wedding goes temporarily blind just before it starts.

Finally, it's over. You scrabble out of the awful garment, get dressed, and join the others.

Cee Cee narrows her eyes at you. "You haven't told me who you're bringing to the wedding."

"Yes, sorry," you say. "I haven't decided yet."

Jane and Cee Cee exchange glances.

"But it's next weekend," Jane says. "Can you let me know by this evening? The calligrapher needs to do the name cards for the tables."

Calligrapher? Oh dear. This is not the laid-back Jane you know and love. Truth is, you haven't decided who you're going to ask to be your plus-one. You haven't told her about Steve yet.

You met him online—one of the few guys who contacted you who didn't have a cocky moniker containing the number 69—and you have to admit that if you showed up with him, you'd create a stir. Steve has the kind of good looks that cause whiplash. And therein lies the problem. On your one and only date with him, you were so busy trying to figure out what the catch was, you barely had a chance to get to know him.

Still, he's a massive improvement on some of the guys you've been out with lately. He has all his own teeth, laughed at your jokes, and when you went for a quick coffee after the movie, he overtipped the waiter (always a good sign). Better still, he wasn't pushy or grabby, leaving you with a chaste but spine-tingling good-night kiss at the end of the evening. Is he just too good to be true?

Or you could go on your own. The wedding wouldn't grind to a halt if every guest wasn't paired up. You know that in spite of her wedding panic, Jane only wants you to be happy, date or no date. And Cee Cee's concern is limited to your plus-one's dietary requirements, shoe size, and whether his personality is suitable for sitting next to the bride's deaf granny or the groom's alkie uncle.

"I'd better get going," Jane says. "I've got a meeting with DJ Salinger."

"Who?" you ask.

a girl walks into a wedding

"The DJ for the reception. Word is he's extremely hot."

"And I'd better head to the airport," Cee Cee says. "Bruno and his date are arriving this afternoon. It's the first time he's been home in years."

"Bruno's bringing a date to the wedding?" you say, remembering the relentless teasing Jane and Cee Cee's brother subjected you to when you were kids. "Who is this woman—some kind of masochist?"

Jane laughs. "Bruno's changed—you're going to be surprised."

"Huh," you say. "Remember when he set my hair on fire? I'm not sure I'm ever going to get over that."

You say your good-byes and leave the bridal shop feeling slightly blue. After that catastrophic bridesmaid dress, you need cheering up. You send an emergency text to your friend Lisa, and she replies within seconds, promising to pick up takeout and a bottle of wine en route to your place.

LISA POURS THE DREGS of the wine into her glass and stuffs the last of the naan into her mouth. "Weddings!" she says. "Why do people put themselves through all that crap?"

You sigh. "It is supposed to be the most important day of your life."

Lisa snorts. "The most stressful day of your life, more like. The whole industry is a giant wedding-planner and florist conspiracy." She runs a hand through her bright pink hair. It's lucky Jane didn't ask her to be a bridesmaid—she'd clash terribly with the new night-mare outfits and the décor palette. "So tell me more about this Steve guy."

"Not much to tell," you say. "He seems nice."

Lisa grimaces. "Nice? Ugh. Sounds boring." Lisa doesn't do nice—or boring. Her last girlfriend was a stuntwoman with more piercings and tattoos than a biker convention.

Your cell phone beeps with a text from Jane:

Plus-one? I NEED TO KNOW!!!!

What to do? Is your best friend's wedding really the place for a second date with Steve? He certainly fits the part; he's handsome and polite, and taking him along would stop Jane's relatives bombarding you with ques-tions about your love life. But you're not sure if you're in the mood for spending the wedding babysitting a guy you barely know, introducing him to everyone and ex-plaining how you met. And you don't really want to tell everyone you've only been on one date with him before. Maybe you could be vague on that point. But more im-portant, do you want Steve to see you in that horror of a bridesmaid dress? It's likely to put him off you forever.

Perhaps you'd be better off going to the wedding on your own. Lisa is going solo after all, and despite her wedding cynicism, she's so much fun to hang out with. If you went on your own, you could really let your hair down with Lisa, and you wouldn't have to stress about whether or not your date was enjoying himself. And you never know who you might meet at the wedding: Didn't Jane say something about the DJ being super hot?

❧ If you want to take Steve to the wedding as your plus-one, go to page 19.

❧ If you want to go to the wedding on your own, go to page 162.

❧ You've decided to go to the wedding with Steve

YOU CAN'T HELP FEELING a bit smug. Choosing Steve to be your date was definitely the right decision.

Here you are, on your way to an early-summer wedding in a red vintage convertible, a gorgeous guy at your side—the star of your very own romantic-movie cliché. You relax back in the car seat, enjoying the feel of the breeze dancing over your skin. It helps that Steve is even better-looking than you remembered. Tall, rangy, and with a smile that meets his eyes every time. You can hardly wait to walk into the hotel on his arm. Jane's eyes will fall out of her head, and even Lisa is sure to be impressed.

There are a few little gaps: You still haven't nailed down exactly what he does for a living—some sort of training for corporate clients is how he put it—but he's employed, says he's well traveled, and he seems to like you a great deal. Sure, you were a little bit concerned at how eagerly he'd agreed to be your plus-one for the wedding, enthusiastically offering to drive you to the country venue—but that worry evaporated when he pulled up outside your place, right on time, in his spectacularly cool car, and ushered you into the passenger seat. He'd even brought you a silk scarf to protect your hair from the wind, and you felt a little like Grace Kelly as he propelled you through the outskirts of the city—people shooting you admiring glances.

So far, so good.

You called the wedding venue—one of those luxury country manor hotels—to book an extra room for him, but now, as you glance at your date in his sunglasses and tight T-shirt, driving with skill and ease, a sneaky part of you is wondering what it might be like to share a room instead.

You leave the city and the traffic behind—Steve has programmed the GPS to take you along the scenic route, and soon you're cruising through rolling countryside down narrow lanes, the hedges full of flowers, the occasional spire of a church punctuating the valleys folded between the sloping hills. You haven't said much to each other—content to let the landscape slide by—but it's a comfortable silence, as if you've known him for ages.

Without taking his eyes off the road, Steve reaches over and weaves his fingers through yours. "Hungry?" he asks.

You were so busy getting ready this morning, you skipped breakfast. A snack in a local pub or diner wouldn't exactly be a hardship. "I could eat," you say.

Helena L. Paige

Steve slows and pulls to the side of the road on the outskirts of a small town. This isn't a cozy local pub. It's a field.

"Why are we stopping here?" you ask.

"Wait and see." He strides around to the trunk and hauls out a picnic basket.

"You packed a picnic?"

"I thought it might be a good plan." He points to a large oak tree set in a clearing in the middle of a field of swaying wheat. A gate marks a public footpath that curves up a slope past the tree. This is too picture-perfect to be true. You look around for the hidden orchestra, but all you can hear are birds and the distant growl of a tractor.

Steve takes your hand and chivalrously helps you through the gate. You stroll along the path, the soft grasses and dandelions on either side tickling your bare legs. When you reach the clearing under the oak, he lays down a mohair blanket, and you kick off your shoes and sink down next to him as he starts unpacking the basket. Unbelievable—sandwiches with the crusts cut off. Chocolate cupcakes. And a bottle of chardonnay in a cooler sleeve.

"You did all this?" you ask.

"Sure."

"Wow. And you've been single for how long?"

He looks a little bashful. "I'm taking my time. But I believe if I put myself out there, stay open to opportunity, the right woman will come along. I just have to keep the faith."

a girl walks into a wedding

He pours you a glass of wine—taking only a splash for himself. "Driving," he shrugs. Mmm, responsible, too. Next he hands you a sandwich, along with a real linen napkin—it's delectable, a simple combination of brown bread, butter, succulent roast chicken, and a hint of fresh rosemary. You sigh in contentment and sip your wine, which is equally good.

The cupcakes are even better, oozing decadent dark-chocolate filling. "Did you make these, too?" you ask, licking your fingers.

"Nah, can't claim the credit there. I have a pretty fantastic baker around the corner from where I live. Their cakes are legendary. I popped in there first thing this morning."

Just as you're thinking that things couldn't get any better, Steve reaches out and tucks a dandelion flower behind your ear. You feel a tingle of warmth in the pit of your belly, and shift a little closer to him. He trails his hand up your arm, slowly stroking your shoulder and neck, his fingers tangling gently in your hair. Then his hand falls away and you're momentarily confused, but he's moving the picnic paraphernalia aside. You shiver with anticipation, the sound of birdsong growing fainter as Steve leans toward you, and there's that delicious moment of knowing that your first real kiss is about to happen. And it doesn't disappoint.

He doesn't rush in, but he's not too tentative, either, and you melt with pleasure as his tongue slides between your lips. You lean back on the soft mohair blanket, wrapping your arms around his neck so that he follows you down, and give yourself over to being thoroughly kissed. The man is a master of the craft, taking his time, combing his hands through your hair. You feel an impressive bulge pressing against your thigh and resist the temptation to reach for it—at least for now.

You're breathless by the time he shifts his mouth to your neck, nuzzling his way down by inches, and as he takes your earlobe gently between his teeth, you explore the honed muscles of his back with your fingers.

He stops and pulls away for a moment, looking into your eyes. Then he eases one of the straps of your sundress off your shoulder.

"Yes," you murmur, sliding your hands down his back and up under the edge of his T-shirt. His skin is warm, and you run your fingertips across his waist and onto his stomach, keen to see if his six-pack feels as good as it looks. It does.

But you're distracted from your own journey by his, as his mouth drops lower, threading kisses past your collarbone and down to the top of your cleavage. He rolls the fabric of your dress down, cups your naked breast in his hand, and slowly, tantalizingly, trails kisses over your nipple. Then you feel his fingers slip the other strap down, exposing both your breasts to the soft, warm air and the pleasure of his mouth.

And then his hand drops lower to slip up under your skirt, teasing along the skin of your thigh, brushing your inner thigh with the tips of his fingers while he wraps his tongue around and around your nipple, then moves to lavish attention on the other one. You sigh as a light breeze plays over your now wet nipple, making you shiver with need.

Then his hand is slipping up over your panties, which are already soaked through, and you part your thighs a little, giving him access. You let out a long breathy gasp as you feel him rubbing the length of your slit from top to bottom. He starts off softly, then increases the pressure of his fingertips over the fabric. First he strokes with just two fingers, and then with all four, applying extra pressure when he reaches your mound, tapping against your clit on every pass. It feels as if that little slip of fabric is the only thing preventing you from coming on the spot.

"Please . . ." you say, tilting up your hips as he rubs the edge of his teeth gently around one of your nipples. At your urging, you feel his fingers just lift the side of your panties, and you know he's about to have at you properly, your breath starts coming a little faster . . .

Your eyes fly open at the sudden roar of an engine, and a tractor chugs into view. Reluctantly, you detach yourself from Steve and whip the straps of your dress up, pulling down your skirt. Steve gently brushes grass off your back. You're tempted to ignore the audience— you were so close to complete satisfaction—but you barely know this guy, so maybe it's a good thing Farmer Brown came along when he did. Who knows how far things might have gone if you hadn't been interrupted?

Back in the car, your head is buzzing delightfully from the glass of wine and your body from Steve's clever fingers and mouth. You're a little itchy from the grass on your bare skin, but you feel sun-kissed and well kissed—and you're anticipating more later. To think you were considering going to the wedding alone!

"Feel like some music?" Steve asks.

"Sure," you say.

He fiddles with his iPod, and next thing, an eighties soft-rock classic blasts out. Not quite what you had in mind.

"Choose something else if you like," he shouts above Foreigner or Chicago or Meatloaf or whatever it is that's blaring out of the speakers and making your ears bleed.

You scroll through his iPod. Oh dear. Several "best of" albums—Celine Dion, Jennifer Rush—the sound track to *The Notebook*, and a Westlife compilation. You feel a twinge of unease. There's no doubt this guy is in touch with his romantic side—maybe too in touch. Still, it's not as if he listens to panpipe music, is it? It could be worse.

It is worse. The next track swells to its crescendo and he starts singing along. He shoots you a meaningful glance while warbling that he really wants to *knooow* what love is. And with taste in music this bad, you're not sure you want to show him.

You smile back tentatively, squirming in your seat. He's just messing with you, surely? Pretending to be cheesy. That has to be it. Thankfully the song changes and he stops singing.

The road weaves past the high gates of several coun-

a girl walks into a wedding

try estates, each more lavishly scenic than the last—you're really in weekend-wedding territory now. You crest a hilltop and round a corner, and your destination slides into view, laid out below you in all its panoramic glory. You knew it would be gorgeous—Jane exploited all of Cee Cee's wedding-planner connections to the max—but this is breathtaking.

A stone mansion basks in the sunshine, with that settled look that comes from being more than a century old. The surrounding gardens stretch in all directions, manicured lawns sweeping toward clumps of trees. A stream running beside a wall divides the gardens from a pasture of grazing sheep. An artfully constructed folly leads the eye up one rise, and behind the mansion, you can see the tower of a chapel made of the same golden stone. As you crunch down the long, graveled drive, the glimmer of a lake behind a row of willows catches your eye. And are those swans on the water? They are.

Steve brings the car to a halt in front of the steps that lead up to the entrance of the manor house, now one of those tremendously exclusive hotels. He leaps out and jogs around the car to open your door. You get out and stretch, gazing out at the lake, enjoying the scent of roses and the quiet. Which is shattered by a cacophony of children's voices, followed by a woman yelling, "Paris! Take your finger out of your nose right now!"

You turn to see Jane's cousin Noeleen and her husband, Dom—for obvious reasons, the pair of them have been Brangelina'd into Domino—and their brood approaching. "Hi!" Noe calls, a toddler wrapped around her ankle. Dom follows, a child clinging to his back like a chimp. You have no idea how they manage their three children—all under seven—without resorting to tranquilizers.

Noe pauses, eyes widening as she takes in Steve. While he shakes hands with Dom, Noe mouths "Wow!" at you. You can't help feeling a flush of pride.

"Mommy! Yodabell wants to go see the swans!"

"Yodabell?" you ask dubiously. Domino's kids all have ridiculous names—you can't remember if the ankle-biter currently tugging at Noe's dress is called Manhattan or Tokyo—but Yodabell is an outrageous moniker, even for this family.

"Yodabell is their pet rat," Dom sighs. "They insisted on bringing him."

On cue, a piebald rat scrambles onto the oldest child's shoulder. You're not a fan of rodents in general, but you feel sorry for this one; it's wearing the same long-suffering expression as Dom.

"Everyone's meeting in the bar for drinks," Noe calls as she and Dom are swept away on a tide of children. "See you in a bit."

"Why don't you check in? I'll park the car around the back and bring in the luggage," Steve says.

You smile at him, and as you turn, he seizes your hand and tugs you back toward him, snaking his arms around your waist. "What, no good-bye kiss?" he murmurs, and your giggle turns into a gasp as he presses his mouth down on yours, his tongue searching for yours once again, his kiss so passionate it takes your breath away. You almost wish you had an audience: Here's you, being kissed like a fifties film star, against a classic convertible outside a magnificent country hotel. And sure, he's got terrible taste in music, but nobody's perfect—and he's a fabulous kisser who makes a mean sandwich.

Eventually, after kissing you thoroughly, twice, Steve lets you go and disappears in the direction of the discreet PARKING FOR GUESTS sign. You float up the wide stone stairs and into the reception area.

Okay, if Cee Cee was responsible for finding this place, you might have to revise your opinion of her taste. The décor is country-house charm, all polished antique furniture and muted chintz, gleaming copper jugs and china vases spilling old-fashioned roses and hydrangeas on every table. A grandfather clock ticks, and sunlight streams through leaded glass onto the Persian rugs on the floor. Down the hall, you catch a glimpse of a Victorian-era-style bar, complete with wood paneling, dark oil paintings, and a deer's antlered head mounted above the baronial fireplace.

You give your name to the receptionist behind the counter and a thought strays into your mind. There's no reason why you couldn't share a room with Steve. It would be pretty forward, but your knees are still wobbly from that kiss outside—you can't help wanting more.

Then again, you don't really know him, do you? Maybe you should take it slowly.

- ✎ If you decide to check in to your own room, go to page 30.

- ✎ If you decide to share a room with Steve, go to page 32.

a girl walks into a wedding

๛ You've decided to check into your own room

YOU'VE CHECKED INTO YOUR own room. After all, there's no law saying you have to sleep in it if you decide to make other arrangements, is there? And if it doesn't work out with Steve, at least you'll have your own space. You follow the receptionist along a paneled hallway, nooks containing antique chairs and writing desks at regular intervals, pausing outside a heavy wooden door.

The receptionist unlocks it and ushers you in.

That's odd—there's a black T-shirt and a pair of jeans draped over the nearest chair. The bathroom door opens, and a man wearing nothing but a towel around his waist emerges whistling.

You stare at each other for a few seconds as the blood rushes to your cheeks. You're tempted to whistle, too— this guy definitely works out. Those are pretty impressive abs, and his muscled arms are decorated with intricate tattoos.

The receptionist flutters behind you, babbling about a room mix-up.

"I don't mind sharing," says Tattoo Guy.

You blush again.

Apologizing nonstop, the receptionist sweeps you back to the entrance desk and clacks at his computer. "I'm so sorry, ma'am," he says, looking as if he's on the verge of tears. "But we're full."

It looks like the decision has been taken out of your hands. You have to share with Steve after all.

❧ Go to page 34.

❧ You've decided to share a room with Steve

THE RECEPTIONIST USHERS YOU along a hall-way adorned with botanical prints and shows you into a huge room dominated by a white four-poster bed. The walls are covered in toile de Jouy paper in soft blues and white. Muslin curtains billow in the breeze float-ing through open French doors that lead onto a balcony. You poke your head into the bathroom, which has an antique wingback chair, enough candles to light up a small church, and a large Jacuzzi in one corner. If this is a regular suite, you can only imagine what the bridal suite must be like.

You thank the receptionist for his help and stroll out onto the balcony, which overlooks the formal rose garden, bordered by precisely barbered lavender bushes. You suck in a deep breath of the dizzyingly scented air and wriggle your shoulders. You could get used to this.

"Hey." A voice breaks into your reverie. There's a tall,

lean, and muscled man on the balcony next to yours. He's wearing nothing but a towel around his narrow waist, and seems completely at ease being half-naked. You wave back, trying not to stare at his impressive biceps, which are looped with tattoos.

"You here for Jane and Tom's wedding, too?" he asks.

You nod. Who is this guy? You thought you'd met all of Jane's friends, and this isn't the kind of man you'd forget, with those dramatic tats and cheekbones that could cut glass. Plus he doesn't look like one of Tom's friends, most of whom are fairly straitlaced, with the exception of Mikey, his best man—a manic macho surgeon with the morals of an alley cat.

"'Scuse the attire," he says. There's the sound of a phone ringing inside his room. He smiles, showing off blindingly white teeth. "Better get that. Catch you later?"

You murmur, "Sure," and step back into the room. Hmm. Maybe you shouldn't be sharing with Steve after all, especially if there's this kind of talent around. You call the receptionist to ask about the extra room you booked for Steve. After much hemming and hawing and a flurry of apologies, he informs you that there's been a mix-up and the extra room you booked has been taken. Oh well, you think. Maybe it was meant to be.

❧ Go to page 34.

a girl walks into a wedding

33

୭ You're sharing a room with Steve

YOU SINK ONTO THE four-poster bed. Pure luxury. You feel a swirl of nerves as you wonder how Steve will react when he realizes you're going to be sharing a room, but after the way he kissed you outside the hotel and what you got up to in that field, you very much doubt he'll be disappointed. And if you're going to be wicked, you've chosen the right place for it, you think, making a snow angel on the giant white bed.

The door opens and Steve enters, your bag slung over his shoulder, a bellhop dragging an enormous suitcase behind him—it's double the size of yours.

Steve hands the bellhop a massive tip and closes the door.

"I hope you don't mind sharing a room," you say.

Steve breaks out his enticing smile again. You move toward him, feeling that familiar buzz in your belly. But instead of getting up close and personal, he drops to his knees and unzips his suitcase. "We're going down to the bar to meet all the other guests now, right?" he says.

You blink. "Right."

"Well, before I meet your friends, I've got something I really want to show you. Prepare yourself, because this is going to blow your mind and open up a whole new way of looking at the world—it's thinking out of the box at its finest."

That sounds ominous. And what can be in that huge suitcase? Women's clothing? Hardcore sex toys? The body of Celine Dion?

He flings open the suitcase. It's filled with DVDs, and horror of horrors, their covers sport a photograph of shirtless Steve in mirrored shades astride a Harley Davidson. He hands you one. The title, *YES U CAN, MAN!* is followed by the words: "Cool Steve's Guide to Surefire Awesomeness: Unlock Your Inner Hidden Potentiality."

Uh-oh.

"Tell you what," he says. "After we've met your friends, how about I see if the hotel has a DVD player we can borrow? I can't wait to show it to you."

You can actually feel the blood draining from your face. He goes on, "It's so great that I'm getting the chance to share this with you and your friends, babe."

Babe. He called you babe. Double uh-oh.

He pulls off his shirt, revealing a tanned stomach with ridged muscles—those same muscles you felt earlier. Muscles that are suddenly not so sexy anymore. He drags a bright yellow T-shirt over his head—the words

a girl walks into a wedding

35

YES U CAN, MAN! blaring in Comic Sans script across the front.

The horror.

"Steve . . . um, the T-shirt," you manage. "You don't think it might be a bit too much?"

"Maybe you're right, babe. Don't want to peak too soon." He smiles at you and slips back into his less offensive shirt. "Shall we?"

YOU CAN HEAR THE sound of laughter and the screeching of Domino's brood coming from the bar area. You're tempted to make a run for it—maybe you can steal Steve's car keys and drive away. As you walk through the lobby, the receptionist signals at you. "Excuse me, ma'am, may I have a word?" His gaze shifts to Steve, and you detect the shadow of lust in his eyes.

"I'll meet you in there," Steve says, giving you a double thumbs-up as he strolls into the bar.

The receptionist drags his eyes away from Steve and turns his attention back to you. "I'm not sure you're still interested"—he shoots another pointed glance in Steve's direction—"but I have a room option for you. It's one half of a family suite, which means you'll have to share a bathroom—"

"I'll take it," you say, snatching the key out of his hand. Right now, you'd sleep on the floor of a barn if you had to.

You take a deep breath and head for the bar. Steve is already in conversation with a stocky guy wearing a dark suit, a tall willowy woman, and an exceptionally good-looking man in a clerical collar.

Jane rushes over to you and gives you a hug. "Is that your date?" she says, gesturing at Steve. "He's *gorgeous*. You are a dark horse."

"Who's he talking to?"

"My brother, of course."

Bruno's back is to you, but it looks like he's grown up quite a bit and lost weight since you last saw him. He turns to look at you as if he can sense your eyes on him, and salutes. Same lopsided grin and shock of black hair as when you were children. He hooks an arm around the tall woman—one of those people who immediately makes you feel disheveled. Graceful, shining hair, no makeup. Not conventionally attractive, but striking.

"That's Cat," Jane says. "She's great. You'll love her. And that's Father Declan," she says, waving at the priest.

"*The* Father Declan? The one you've had a completely forbidden crush on for years?"

Jane laughs. "Do you blame me?"

You don't. He's slightly rumpled in that rakish way, and his eyes are fringed with thick black eyelashes—the kind that always made your gran say, "God put in those eyes with a sooty finger." The lines on his face suggest that he does a lot of smiling, and right now he's roaring with laughter at something Steve is telling him. You hope he's laughing with Steve and not at him.

On the other side of the room, Lisa grimaces at you from where she's been cornered by Cee Cee—who is no doubt rattling off the finer details of the napkin-cum-dress décor. You wave hello to Tom, Jane's fiancé, who's leaning against the bar with a man dressed in a crumpled khaki shirt. Mikey—the best man.

"Mikey's single again," Jane says. You give her a sharp look. "Don't worry, even if you hadn't shown up with a date who makes Ryan Gosling look like the Elephant Man, he knows you're not the type of girl who would fall for his lame pickup lines."

No, you're the type of girl who comes to a wedding with a complete stranger who just happens to be a rabid wannabe self-help guru.

Mikey gives you a lazy, assessing smile. On paper, he's the sort of guy who would be the star of hospital romance novels—a maverick who travels the world with Doctors Without Borders. In reality, you know that despite his noble-sounding job, he's an unrepentant womanizer with severe income-tax issues.

"I'd better mingle," Jane says. "I can't wait to get to know Steve better!" And it looks like Jane isn't the only one. Jane's aunt Lauren, a foxy woman of a certain age who achieved notoriety in the sixties and beyond as a model and avant-garde photographer, is obviously circling, twirling her long black cigarette holder. And several of the waitstaff—both male and female—are also hovering rather closely. If you could only tape Steve's mouth shut, you might actually be enjoying this.

"Hello again." You turn to see the tattooed guy you encountered earlier. He looks just as good in his clothes as he did in his towel. "Bride or groom?"

"Just a guest," you say.

He laughs. "I mean, are you a friend of the bride or the groom?"

"Sorry! Both, I guess. You?"

"I'm handling the music for the wedding."

"Oh! You must be DJ Salinger." Jane wasn't lying when she said he was hot. "How come you're here for the whole weekend?"

"Tom's my vet. He's helped me out loads of times in the past. I have an elderly cat who's prone to middle-of-the-night emergencies, and this is my way of repaying the favor. And when he suggested I spend the weekend here, I thought, why not?"

"Is Salinger really your last name?"

"Nah. I got an MFA in English before I studied sound engineering, thought it would be a cool alias. You can call me JD."

He waves at the doors leading out onto the veranda with spectacular views of lawns and trees. "Feel like getting some air?"

Steve is still regaling Aunt Lauren, Bruno, Father Declan, and Bruno's perfect girlfriend with heaven knows what. Should you go over there to make sure he isn't trying to shove self-help psychobabble down their throats? Or would you rather visit a town named denial, and chat with the DJ?

❧ If you decide to talk to the DJ, go to page 40.

❧ If you try to corral Steve before he embarrasses you completely, go to page 43.

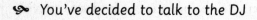

❧ You've decided to talk to the DJ

JD SNARES A GLASS of bubbles from a passing waiter and hands it to you before escorting you toward the veranda. Someone should frame those cheekbones, and his lips are so full and sensuous you want to run your thumb along them. It also doesn't hurt that he's the kind of edgy-hot guy Lisa would approve of.

"So . . . you here with anyone?" he asks.

The temptation to fudge the truth is immense. But you've seen those movies where the main character lies and gets herself into endless trouble. "I'm with a friend."

"Boyfriend?"

"God, no."

"Interesting." JD holds your eyes for a long second, and it's suddenly hard to swallow.

"And you?" you finally manage. "Are you here with someone?"

He smiles lazily, and a dimple pops up next to those kissable lips. "Not yet."

"I *thought* it was you, Stinky," a voice says from behind. You turn to see Bruno and his girlfriend approaching.

"Stinky?" JD cocks an eyebrow.

"Bruno used to call me Stinky when we were kids," you say, more than a little annoyed. "He used to get his kicks from pushing me into cow pies."

Bruno laughs. "You got your revenge," he says to you. "She drowned my G.I. Joe in the toilet," he explains to JD and Cat.

Cat smiles at you and introduces herself. "We've just been talking to the most hilarious guy," she says.

"Really?" you say through gritted teeth. Before you can explain that you barely know him, a familiar voice yodels, "Babe! There you are." Steve bounces up to you, trailed by Aunt Lauren. "Lauren here is dying to see one of my DVDs."

Your face burning, you introduce him to JD, who's looking at you quizzically.

"DVDs?" Bruno asks.

"Don't ask," you mutter.

With a glance at you and Steve, JD excuses himself, giving you a regretful smile as he leaves.

"Are you coming to the bachelor party tonight?" Bruno asks Steve. "We're heading out for a few drinks, nothing major."

Steve clicks his fingers. "Sure! Hey, I've had a great

idea. I'll be back in a minute!" He spins on his heel and jogs out.

"That's the guy we were talking to earlier," Cat says. "I didn't realize you two were together."

Bruno smirks at you—he clearly hasn't changed. Perhaps now would be a good time to rescue Lisa, who's still having her ear talked off by Cee Cee—anything to get away from this.

❧ Go to page 45.

Helena L. Paige

🪢 You've decided to corral Steve before he embarrasses you

YOU SMILE REGRETFULLY AT the DJ. "Excuse me. I must just . . ." you mutter as you sidle up to the small group surrounding Steve. Thank goodness—they're talking about cars.

"Hi, Stinky!" Bruno greets you.

You bite back your instinctive "Hi, asshole!" retort.

"Stinky?" Bruno's girlfriend, Cat, asks, giving you a smile.

"It's what he used to call me when we were kids," you say, clenching your fists. "Although to be honest, he was the one who reeked a bit."

"So, Steve," Aunt Lauren purrs, "tell me more about yourself. What do you do for a living?"

"Steve!" you jump in, desperate to change the subject. "Um . . . maybe we can find a DVD player? Remember, you wanted to show me something."

Bruno raises an eyebrow. "DVD? Party favor for the bachelor party later?"

"My dear, *please* tell me you've made a sex tape," says Aunt Lauren, widening her eyes in delight. Father Declan looks as if he's suppressing a smile.

You grimace. "I—"

"Speaking of the bachelor party, I've had a great idea!" Steve says. "Babe, you're going to love this! Wait here a moment . . ." He hurries away.

Lisa is waving at you, clearly desperate to be rescued from Cee Cee's clutches. Bruno smirks at you as you make your excuses and slink away to join her.

 Go to page 45.

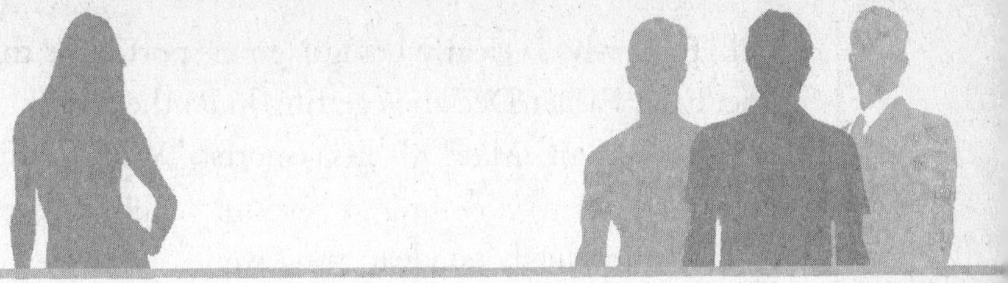

You go over to rescue Lisa from Cee Cee

You join Lisa and Cee Cee, who shoots air kisses around your head, then drifts off to talk to Domino, who are juggling stiff drinks, a pet rat, toddlers, and canapés with the skill of Cirque du Soleil performers. Bruno and Cat stroll out of the room arm in arm, chatting nonstop to each other.

"Was that Steve I just saw running out of here?" Lisa asks. "Nice, *boring* Steve?"

"Yeah. Only he's not as boring as you might think. Unfortunately. You should see what he keeps in his suitcase."

Lisa's eyes gleam. "Oooh. Sounds fun. Tell all."

You're about to fill her in when Steve bursts into the room with a bundle of bright yellow T-shirts in his arms.

"Guys! I thought these would be perfect for tonight!" he shouts, and you watch, appalled, as he hands them out. Mikey chuckles, strips off his shirt, and pulls one over his head. Tom, who is clearly being a good sport, does the same. Even Father Declan is getting in on the action.

"'Yes U Can, Man!'?" Lisa snorts. "Who *is* this guy?"

"I have absolutely no idea," you say.

With Steve occupied, you make an excuse about freshening up and sneak away to your new room, a single that shares a bathroom with the suite next door.

The room is a little less luxurious than the one you were going to share with Steve, but you don't care. You collapse onto the bed. Perhaps Lisa will help you work out how to escape the whole Steve situation. She's extricated herself from more tricky relationships than you've had hot dinners.

You don't want to be cruel; Steve doesn't seem like such a bad person. But the self-help stuff is more than enough to wipe out anything you felt for him, however good a kisser he is. You should have known those looks were too good to be true.

The last thing you feel like doing now is going back to the bar and avoiding Steve, and it's true that you feel dusty after the long drive, so you decide to wash away your troubles instead.

You walk into a huge marbled room, with a claw-footed bath set at an angle in one corner and an enormous, luxurious shower in the other.

If you want a bubble bath, go to page 47.

If you want a shower, go to page 50.

❧ You decide to have a bubble bath

YOU RUN A BATH, emptying every drop of the complimentary bubble bath soap into the old-fashioned tub, and strip off your clothes. You climb in and close your eyes, sighing as the hot water and jasmine-scented foam envelop you.

Heaven.

You spill water over the side as you hear the sound of a door opening. Dammit—you completely forgot to lock the door connecting to the other room.

You slide under the water, but you can't hold your breath forever. You surface, coming face-to-face with a pair of dark eyes and a shock of black hair.

"I thought it was you, Stinky," Bruno says.

Fortunately the bubbles hide most of your nakedness, but they're dissolving fast.

"Do you mind?" you snap, snatching a facecloth and

covering your breasts as best you can with the small square of fabric.

"I don't mind, actually," Bruno says, brazenly checking you out. "You're in my bathroom, after all."

"*Our* bathroom." You explain the mix-up with the room.

"But I thought you came here with your boyfriend?"

"He's not my boyfriend."

"I thought I heard him calling you 'babe.'"

You really don't feel like going into the short history of your and Steve's relationship with your childhood nemesis. You scrabble for an explanation. "It's . . . his nickname for me. Um . . . after Babe. You know, the one from the movie, the pig that thinks it's a sheep."

Bruno bursts out laughing. "So you've progressed from being Stinky to a pig?"

"Yes," you say haughtily.

"Well, I'd keep Steve on a short leash, if I were you. Aunt Lauren thinks he's the best-looking guy she's ever seen. And you know what that means."

"I'd forgotten she was going to be here. At least with her around, things won't be dull."

"I'll say. No well-endowed waiter will be safe." He sits down on the closed toilet lid. "So what have you been doing since I saw you last, apart from collecting ridiculous nicknames?"

You fill him in briefly on a few career highlights. For some reason it feels completely natural to be swapping notes about your lives while naked in the bath. Bruno tells you about his work as a sitcom screenwriter, launch-

Helena L. Paige

ing into an amusing and scurrilous story about an A-list actor and Scientologist who made a cameo appearance on one of his shows. "None of the crew or extras was allowed to look him in the eye," he says. "And everyone over five nine had to clear the set so that he'd feel taller. I didn't get the day off, of course. The curse of being a short dude."

He smiles self-consciously, which is at odds with the brash Bruno you remember from your childhood. Could he have changed? Lost some of his cockiness along with the puppy fat? You almost say something about size not mattering, but decide to change the subject instead.

"So tell me about Cat," you say. "How did you two meet?"

❧ Go to page 53.

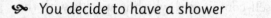

❧ You decide to have a shower

YOU STEP INTO THE shower and turn on the water—it comes shooting at you from multiple angles, and you revolve slowly so that the water from the jets hits you all over.

Slowly you start soaping yourself, your hands running over your breasts and then down to your thighs, the heady smell of jasmine filling the bathroom.

You reach for the sachet you brought with you—an expensive hair hydrating mask, or masque, according to the label—which instructs you to massage it into your hair and leave in for precisely eight minutes before shampooing it out. You tear the sachet open with your teeth and apply the creamy contents to your head, turning off the taps while you work it into your scalp. You bend down to take a closer look at the thigh-height jets. Hmm, you could do a lot with one of those in eight minutes.

You hear a creak and the door to the connecting room

opens. Shit, you had assumed it was locked. You shoot up straight, trying to cover your nakedness with your hands, doubly embarrassed not only at being caught in the shower, but at your naughty thoughts—you're sure they're etched all over your face.

Oh no. It's Bruno, and he's heading for the sink, humming under his breath. He squeezes toothpaste onto his toothbrush and starts brushing his teeth. You stand frozen to the spot, aware that the towels are on the rail on the other side of the bathroom. When Bruno sees you reflected in the mirror, he starts and swears, then turns around. Your eyes lock for several seconds.

"What are you doing in my bathroom?" he says.

"*Our* bathroom! And would you mind turning around!" you yelp, your pricey hair goo dripping slowly down your face.

Bruno laughs. "Don't panic, Stinky. I can't see anything. Unfortunately."

He's right. The shower door is conveniently frosted from about upper thigh to chest height. But it still feels weird to be standing naked with him only a few feet away.

"And what do you mean 'our bathroom'?" he asks.

"The only single room available was the one next door, and it's connected to your bathroom," you explain.

"How come you aren't sharing a room with your boyfriend?"

You frown. "Why do you think?"

"I don't know, he seems cool. And he looks like the

51

love child of David Beckham and Daniel Craig—isn't that what women want?"

Bruno looks momentarily downcast. You've always suspected he felt a bit self-conscious about his looks. As a teenager he was pimply, a bit overweight, and short. He's grown since then, lost the pimples and most of the weight, but as looks go, he's not in Steve's league by any stretch of the imagination.

"Looks aren't everything," you say, feeling a pang for him. For a second, you forget that you're naked, and that Bruno used to be your sworn enemy. "I've got another seven minutes to wait while this conditioner does its work. You may as well fill me in on what you've been up to."

Bruno sits down on the closed toilet seat and starts telling you about his job as a screenwriter for several comedy series. His imitation of an actor who demanded to know what his character's "motivation" was for spilling a cup of coffee actually makes you laugh out loud.

"So what about your personal life?" you ask. "Cat seems really nice."

🌢 Go to page 53.

❧ Cat joins you and Bruno in the bathroom

 As IF ON CUE, the door opens and Cat enters, dressed only in her underwear—matching, expensive, lacy underwear at that. You wonder if it's possible that by the end of the weekend, you will have seen every single guest in a state of undress.

She blinks as she takes in the spectacle of you nude, albeit partially screened, and Bruno perched on the toilet seat.

"Am I interrupting something?" she asks.

"No, no!" You hastily explain the room debacle. She doesn't seem especially concerned that Bruno has been in here for far longer than should be necessary to discover a naked woman in their bathroom. She's clearly not the jealous type.

Cat sits down on Bruno's lap, and you register the easy familiarity between them. She asks you about Bruno's childhood, and you spend a few minutes filling in the gorier details. She throws him a play punch when you tell her about the time he set your hair on fire, killing the blaze by throwing a jug of lemonade over your head.

"I'd better rinse off and get dressed," you say, when there's a pause in the conversation.

"Go ahead," Bruno says invitingly. Cat play-punches him again, but they leave together.

You're surprised how much you enjoyed chatting with Bruno. You suspect he's still a bit of a bastard, but at least now he's an entertaining bastard. And Cat is the sort of woman you wouldn't mind hanging out with. That could have been so much more embarrassing than it actually was.

You finish washing your hair, wrap yourself in a thick and thirsty bath towel the size of a sail, then pad into your room, having snagged the complimentary body lotion in the bathroom—you remember reading that it's best stroked on while your skin is still warm and damp. You crawl onto the bed, still wrapped in your fluffy towel, squeeze a blob of lotion into the palm of one hand, then start to apply it to your bare legs. It smells of freesia, citrus, and something tropical, and you sigh as you relax.

Between the long drive and your discoveries about Steve, you could do with a power nap. You lie back against the pillows, telling yourself you'll just close your eyes for a couple of minutes.

As you're about to drift off, there's a soft tap at the door. You clutch your towel a little closer and prop yourself up on one elbow, hoping that Steve hasn't tracked you down. But it's JD's head that appears around the door. "Can I come in?" he asks. "I don't want to disturb you."

You're puzzled, but intrigued, especially when he slides around the door wearing only a pair of jeans, his magnificent torso and tattoos on display. "Have they mixed up our rooms?" you ask, wrenching your eyes from his chest to his face.

"No, nothing like that. I'm just planning my playlist, and although I've got the request for the first dance, I thought you'd be the best person to ask if there are any other songs that have special meaning for Jane and Tom."

Your mind goes blank, but then you remember. "It's old-school, I know, but Jane loves 'You Got a Friend.' The Carole King version."

"Thanks." He makes no move to leave and you look inquiringly at him.

His eyes stray to the body lotion on the bedside table. "Seeing as you did me a favor . . . could I be of service to you?" He strolls over to the bed and grins down at you.

You're completely thrown, very aware that you're warm, drowsy, and stark-naked under your towel.

"For instance, you might need someone to rub this lotion onto your skin," JD goes on.

You take a long look at him. You really should ask him to leave immediately, but instead, you find yourself extending an arm toward him, your hand falling open.

"You can start with my arm," you say, almost imperiously.

JD's teeth flash as he sits down on the edge of the bed next to you, lifts your arm, and lays it across his lap.

Then he slathers cream across his hands, rubbing them together. "Relax and don't worry about a thing," he murmurs, as he grips the top of your arm gently with both hands, forming a cuff of fingers which he pulls firmly and slowly down the length of your arm. When he reaches your hand, he uncurls the palm and gets to work with both his thumbs, kneading across the fleshy pad of your hand beneath your thumb, and pressing the sensitive spots just below each finger.

You make a faint noise of pleasure and approval, and relax still more deeply, lying back against the pillows as he repeats the entire movement. Then he moves around to the other side of the bed and begins to work on the other arm. This time, once he's repeated the pull-knead maneuver, he lifts your hand to his lips and delicately nips at each fingertip in turn, the slightest press of tooth and tongue.

Your gasp is audible, as the warm sensation elicited by his stroking hands is amplified by a distinctive tug in your lower belly. You wriggle very slightly in your towel cocoon, feeling heat rise to the surface of your skin.

JD doesn't seem to notice. He applies more of the fragrant lotion to his hands, moves lower down the bed, slides his hands under your calf and foot, and lifts your leg slightly. You can't help a flare of anticipation as he tugs it to one side, opening you up a little, but he seems intent on massaging your feet, and you almost whimper as his long, strong fingers probe deeply into your instep in small, circular movements. Then he slides his hands over and around your ankle, caressing the circle of sensitive flesh just beneath the anklebone.

"That feels so good," you say, breaking the spell of silence—apart from the sound of your breathing—that has fallen.

"According to reflexologists, this part of the foot corresponds with, er, the female parts," JD says smoothly.

At his words, you feel an unmistakable pulse in the said female parts, which becomes more insistent as JD switches his attentions to your other foot. Part of you wants to drift as he rubs and soothes and strokes, and part of you is tense with anticipation, wondering where those clever fingers will wander next.

And then he slides both hands up one of your legs, kneading the calf firmly, then stroking the soft spot behind your knees with exquisite delicacy. You know it's wanton, but you soften your legs, letting them fall a little farther apart, as he nudges the edge of the towel up, creeping up your thigh with maddening slowness.

He lifts your entire leg and flexes it, placing it back on the bed in a bent position. The towel falls away from your thigh, with just one fold falling between your legs, all that's shielding your heated pussy from view.

Still moving slowly, his hand travels the length of your inner thigh, stopping just short of your pussy, his thumb traveling in lazy, teasing circles. You can feel the wetness flooding your pussy lips, the syrupy sensation of fullness in your pelvis, his fingers just an inch away, you're mad for him to slide them home—and then he

a girl walks into a wedding

57

shifts, switches sides, and starts all over again with your other leg.

You can't help it, a little noise of frustration escapes you, and his hands still at once. "Would you like me to stop?"

"God, no," you groan, and give yourself over to the slow torture of his hands traveling gradually up your leg, now feathering your other thigh, closer, closer, almost grazing against your pussy—and then he stops again.

This time, you arch your back and lift your hips with frustration, and with the movement, your towel starts to slide open, exposing your breasts.

"Would you like me to—?" JD pauses.

"Oh yes, please!" you beg, casting all caution to the winds.

This time, there's no teasing: He places his warm, supple hands directly onto your breasts. They're still slightly oiled from the lotion, and he massages your flesh firmly but gently, rubbing in circular movements. Your nipples pop against his warm palms, and he grunts with satisfaction. Through your half-open eyes, you see his Adam's apple moving in his strong lean throat, and with a thrill, you realize he's as excited as you are.

Then his hands slide around your back, one coming up to cup your head as he kisses you, tentatively at first, his lips just grazing against yours, his tongue pressing hesitantly, then retreating.

And you open up your mouth to him, seizing his head and winding your fingers in his hair, and you take long drafts of each other's mouths, the soft wet noises of tongue against tongue the only sounds in the room apart from your accelerated breathing.

Still holding your head with one hand, he shifts his long lithe body alongside yours on the bed and trails his free hand down from the top of your chest, between your breasts, slowly over your rib cage and tummy, pausing to dip a finger into your belly button, before finally coming to rest on your mound.

"Please," you say again, tilting your pelvis up against his hand, and at last he strokes down between your swollen wet folds, spreading them open, exploring and teasing, his middle finger nudging the opening of your cunt, just dipping in, until you raise your hips and his finger slides up and in, and you both gasp with mingled hunger and satisfaction.

The two of you kiss again, his tongue mimicking the slow movements of his finger inside you until you move your head slightly and capture his earlobe with your teeth.

"I can't wait any longer," you whisper, and he dips one hand into his jeans pocket and pulls out a condom, then moves away from you momentarily to strip off his jeans. He has the most magnificent bottom, neat and tight, but you only get to admire it for a few seconds before he kneels between your legs, the tattoos on his skin rippling as he braces an arm on either side of your shoulders.

He seizes a pillow and threads it under your hips, raising the core of you up to him, and you wrap your legs around his waist, presenting his erection with a

a girl walks into a wedding

bull's-eye. He buries the tip of his cock between your pussy lips, and once again, you both groan as you push up and against him, and he slides in, pressing deeper and deeper as you clutch at him, digging your fingers into the strong muscles of his back, your feet pressed against his buttocks.

His cock isn't just a generous length, it's also thick, and you can feel yourself stretching around him, clasping him intimately, your bodies settling and adjusting to the angle and each other. He kisses you again, lingeringly, then tucks his chin into the curve between your neck and shoulder as he begins to thrust, slowly at first, grunting with each stroke.

There's something about the angle of your hips, or maybe it's because you're so relaxed; each time he pushes into you, every nerve ending in your body thrums as he stretches the cushiony walls deep inside you. You know you're heading for a huge, effortless orgasm, and all you have to do is lie back and let it wash through you . . . one more thrust, one more, just one more . . . and you explode in JD's arms, your back arching so strongly you lift him with you, your pussy clenching and unclenching around his cock as wave after wave of intense pleasure radiates out from your pelvis all the way to the roots of your hair.

Your orgasm triggers him off, and with a shout, he comes as well, every muscle in his body tightening seconds before he collapses bonelessly in your arms, then slowly rolls off you, your limbs still tangled together.

There are long minutes in which all you can hear is

each other's ragged breathing. You tuck your head into the hollow of his shoulder, and reach out an idle finger to stroke the tattoos on his arms. The symbols look vaguely Celtic—now that you're looking more closely, that seems to be a dragon, but it's wavering and dissolving.

Puzzled, you look up at JD's face, but it's Bruno's eyes that are looking back at you. What's going on? And why is someone beating out a tattoo on a drum?

YOU BLINK, AND THIS time when you open your eyes, you're alone on your bed, still wrapped in a towel, and smelling of frangipani or something equally exotic. The drumroll is a hammering on the door. You've been asleep and dreaming, for far longer than you intended— judging by the golden light outside the window, dusk is approaching. You get up on legs that still feel wonderfully loose and lazy, and check the peephole.

It's Cee Cee.

"I need your help," she says, pushing past you into the room. "I'm having a crisis! I booked the hotel spa for this evening for all of us girls—pampering and all that. But they've had an unfortunate waxing incident and have canceled. What are we going to do now? The receptionist says the local pub has a karaoke night, but that could be too low-rent. Otherwise, we could stay in and have a girls-only pajama party. What do you think we should do?"

Excellent, you think, knuckling your eyes, trying to

clear away the remnants of your dream. You understand why the handsome DJ showed up on cue, but what was Bruno doing in your head? In real life, however, the bachelorette party will solve your Steve problem for now—he'll be out at the bachelor party, so you'll be able to delay the awkward but inevitable "I'm just not that into you" conversation for one night at least. The question is, do you feel like an evening of bad cover numbers and cheap tequila shots, or a night in with the girls, chucking lurid lingerie around?

❧ If you decide that an evening of karaoke is the way to go, go to page 63.

❧ If you'd prefer a girls' night in, go to page 71.

THE KARAOKE NIGHT IS exactly what you expected: a country pub with a microphone, a makeshift stage, and a balding DJ behind a plywood box in one corner.

You managed to escape the hotel without having any alone time with Steve. As he and the group of yellow T-shirted guys headed out for their own night of fun, he tried to kiss you on the mouth, but you managed to swerve so that it landed on your cheek. Bruno, who was wearing his YES U CAN! T-shirt over a long-sleeved black shirt, gave you an unreadable look, and you didn't see any sign of JD.

But now you need to put your Steve concerns aside and make sure Jane enjoys her last night as an unmarried woman. She's looking strained and is ordering cocktails and shooters in rather excessive quantities.

You join her at the bar, where Lisa and Cat are doing

their first round of tequila shots. Aunt Lauren is leaning on the counter, chatting up the bartender, who's almost young enough to be her grandson. And judging by the look on his face, she might just have scored. At least someone's getting lucky tonight. You think wistfully about JD and his intriguing tats. You wouldn't mind finding out if that ink extends to other parts of his body, but there's no chance of that now. He obviously assumes that you and Steve are a couple.

Jane knocks back one shot, then another. You follow suit, feeling the alcohol hitting your system and flooding your veins. You watch as Cee Cee and Noe blast out "I Will Survive" at the top of their lungs. Lisa and Cat are deep in conversation, their heads close together.

"You think I'm doing the right thing?" Jane asks.

"No. Karaoke is never a good idea."

"I mean . . . with all the wedding preparations, I sort of haven't had time to think . . . if marriage is what I really want."

What could have sparked this off? You like Tom; he's kindhearted, a decent guy, but truth is, you're worried that he might be a little bit, well—as Lisa would say—fucking boring. "But you and Tom have been together since college."

"That's the problem—I haven't been with anyone else. Don't get me wrong, Tom is wonderful, it's just . . . What if there's someone else out there I'm supposed to be with?"

You're out of your depth here, but you tell yourself

that it's normal for the bride to get cold feet before the wedding. Isn't it?

The microphone whines, making you wince. "This is for the special woman in my life," a man's voice croons. Uh-oh. You know that voice.

You turn slowly, feeling the kind of dread usually reserved for when you find a spider in the bath. Steve's onstage, microphone in hand, about to launch into what sounds horribly like "Unchained Melody." What is he doing here? He must have slipped away from the bachelor party. Still, as his voice throbs on the first "da-ar-ar-ar-ling," sending shudders down your spine, a tiny fragment of your brain acknowledges that he is possibly the only man in the world who looks good in a yellow T-shirt.

Lisa looks over to you and mouths, "Oh my god."

"Isn't that Steve?" Jane asks. Aunt Lauren is whooping in front of the stage, the young bartender forgotten.

You feel an overwhelming urge to flee. But how can you abandon Jane at her bachelorette party? You're supposed to be her best friend!

But . . . can you stand the embarrassment of Steve serenading you?

☙ If you decide to stay and face the music,
   go to page 66.

☙ If you make a run for it, go to page 68.

🎕 You've decided to stay and face the music

JANE MAY BE DRUNK, but she's not insensitive to your plight. Steve is trying to spot you in the crowd, and it won't be long before he does. He'll probably ask you to come up onstage with him, and you're not nearly drunk enough for that sort of experience to be anything but excruciating.

"Come on," she says. "Let's get out of here. I've had enough, anyway."

You both head for the ladies' room and then dart out to the parking lot. Cee Cee has arranged a car to collect you all after the pub closes, but that's at least an hour away. Fortunately, a taxi from the nearby village is dropping off an inebriated couple, and Jane staggers toward it.

You get in and ask the driver to take you to your hotel.

"You're in luck," he says. "I was just about to call it a night."

You ask Jane if she wants to discuss her cold-feet

issues, but she mumbles something about talking it over tomorrow. She falls asleep on your shoulder in the cab, and when you reach the manor, you have to half carry her to her room. She's going to have a raging hangover when she wakes up, so you persuade her to take an aspirin and down a glass of water.

You make yourself a cup of tea from the complimentary pack on top of the minibar, sit with her until she falls asleep, then head to your room.

You round the corner and stop dead in your tracks as you spot a figure in a yellow T-shirt knocking at your door.

"Babe? Babe? You in there?"

You're really not up for a tricky conversation with Steve right now. What to do?

ꙮ If you go outside for some fresh air while you wait for him to leave, go to page 73.

ꙮ If you sneak down to the bar for a nightcap, go to page 84.

❧ You've decided to make a run for it

"JUST HEADING TO THE bathroom," you shout over the caterwauling.

Feeling guilty for abandoning your friend, you slink into the night. You send Jane a quick text explaining why you've absconded. But now what? You need to get back to the hotel. You try calling for a taxi, but you're in the middle of nowhere, and the number for the nearby village's only taxi service goes straight to voice mail.

You have no choice but to walk. On the plus side, it's only a mile or so, and you could do with the exercise and fresh night air after downing all that tequila. You slip off your heels and walk barefoot down the side of the road, enjoying the feel of cool grass between your toes.

It's a warm evening, but the moon is shrouded in cloud and there's nothing to light your way. You hope you don't end up falling in a ditch.

❧ You've decided to stay at the hotel and
have an all-girls' pajama party

AS PAJAMA PARTIES GO, this one hasn't been
half bad. Aunt Lauren showed up with several bottles of
Moët that she'd wheedled out of the hotel manager, and
has been regaling you all with tales of her life as a photographer in the swinging sixties. You've also discovered
that Cat, Bruno's girlfriend, is not only extremely nice,
but has a string of major accomplishments to her name.
She's published a novel and sailed around the world—
and she managed to reveal these facts while coming
across as self-deprecating and funny. The only mystery is
what she's doing with Bruno.

The evening is winding down. The other guests left
hours ago, Lisa and Cat are sitting on one side of the bed,
engrossed in conversation, and Cee Cee and Noe, both
blitzed, are singing a Beyoncé number. Aunt Lauren is
out on the balcony smoking a joint.

Only Jane is looking maudlin.

"What's up with you?" you ask.

She shrugs exaggeratedly—she's more than a little drunk. "Think I'm having a bit of . . . whatchoocallits—cold meats." She hiccups.

"Cold feet? About marrying Tom?" This is not good. You like Tom—what's not to like? He's kind-hearted, stable, and he's a vet. But you have to admit he's not the most exciting guy in the world.

"Yesh. No . . . I dunno." She hiccups again. "Don't mind me. Jusht tipshy." She stands up and sways. You'd better help her to bed.

You say good night to the others and guide her to her room.

"You want to talk about this some more?" you ask.

"Tomorrow," she slurs, collapsing onto the bed. You make her drink a couple of glasses of water, tuck her in, and make your way to your own room.

You turn the corner and freeze—there's a familiar figure in a yellow T-shirt knocking on your door.

"Babe? We need to talk." Oh no—it's Steve. You are so not ready for this.

What do you do now?

❧ If you head outside for some fresh air while you wait for him to leave, go to page 73.

❧ If you sneak down to the bar for a nightcap, go to page 84.

∾ You've headed out for some air while you wait for Steve to leave

FEELING LIKE A COWARD for not facing Steve and telling him that your future together is a definite "NO U CAN'T" scenario, you flee through the reception area and out the French doors that lead to the hotel gardens.

It's a gorgeous night, the air warm and balmy. The clouds clear, and moonlight dances over the lake. You wander down to it, skirting its edge, pausing to dip your fingers in the water. You're almost tempted to strip off your clothes and dive in, but where's the fun in skinny-dipping by yourself?

"Babe?" You turn and see a silhouetted figure standing on the hotel veranda, peering around.

Shit. You scurry into the nearby summerhouse, an

elegant structure containing boxes of florist's supplies, dozens of stacked slatted chairs, and several lounge chairs. It looks out over the water, and it's private and peaceful—the perfect spot to hide out for a little while.

❧ Go to page 75.

Helena L. Paige

🙡 You've taken refuge in the summerhouse

 YOU HEAR FOOTSTEPS APPROACHING and the sound of whispered voices. Oh, shit. Has Steve rounded up reinforcements? You look around wildly, then duck behind a latticed screen in the corner of the summerhouse.

Floorboards creak, then you hear the fizz of a match and catch the scent of candle wax. You peek through the lattice and see two figures, a man and a woman, lighting several of the extra tealight candles Cee Cee bought for the wedding, "just in case." As the light blooms, you recognize JD and a waitress from the get-together in the bar.

This is awkward—clearly they have romantic intentions, and you don't want to be a fly on the wall—but how are you going to extricate yourself? Perhaps if you stay quiet, they'll go away.

- If you decide to stay hidden and hope they leave, go to page 77.

- If you decide to get out of there somehow, go to page 82.

≫ You decide to stay hidden and hope they leave

YOU CROUCH DOWN AND cross your fingers, hoping they'll go away. But your hopes are dashed by the sounds of quickened breathing, gentle moans, kissing, and the rustle of clothing being discarded. You apply an eye to the lattice—you're not spying on them, you just want to know what stage they're at. If they're still decent, maybe you can emerge, making some excuse. You could tell them you're doing a study on the nocturnal habits of swans—anything that might explain why you're skulking by the water's edge in the middle of the night.

But it's too late. They're both already shirtless, and you can't tear your eyes away, even though you know you should. The candles cast dramatic shadows and warm lights on their skin, and JD's tattoos ripple with a life of their own. His body is hard and lithe, while hers is voluptuous, with skin that looks almost velvet-soft. The contrast between their different textures and shapes as they press their bodies together is amazing.

By now they're entwined and kissing passionately, the soft sounds and murmurs heightened in the still night. You're sweating with embarrassment—and, if you're honest, with something else, too.

Look away, look away, you tell yourself, but you keep watching as they move together like dancers, now helping each other out of their remaining clothes, pausing only to nuzzle and kiss each other. As you stare, JD bends his head to the waitress's apple-shaped breasts, and she tosses her head back, the line of her throat catching the flickering light, her hair, released from its earlier neat bun, rippling down her back. His strong hands sweep down to the curves of her bottom, cupping her buttocks, his fingers clearly outlined as they knead and sink into the lush skin.

Then he sweeps her up into his arms and carries her to a lounge chair, laying her down and straddling her. You don't know whether to be thrilled or appalled— you're going to have a ringside view for the next round. Things have gone way too far for you to reveal yourself now. You're along for the ride, like it or not, and much as you hate to confess it, part of you likes it very much indeed.

Next time you look, JD is lowering himself between the waitress's legs, and they both groan as he enters her. You've never watched two people having sex before, and it's strangely beautiful, like watching an ancient pagan rite, but incredibly sensual, too.

JD begins to move rhythmically, slowly at first, his partner's head tilting back with each stroke, her hands clenching and unclenching on his shoulders, her voice catching in little breathy noises.

There's no fudging this—you're shamelessly watching two relative strangers getting it on, and worse, you're panting almost as hard as they are. You touch your damp neck, then slide your hand down and over your breast, feeling your heart pounding under the skin. Your nipple is rock hard, and it's not just the night air that's responsible.

You can't help yourself—you slide your other hand under your skirt and into your panties, which are wet through. Your fingers are trembling from a mix of anxiety, desire, and the strangeness of the experience—you're doing something forbidden, but as you slide your index finger between your warm, slick pussy lips and gasp, you know there's no turning back.

Meanwhile, the couple has picked up the pace. You gaze hypnotized at JD's muscular buttocks as they rise and fall, faster and harder, imagining that you're the one he's thrusting into, that you're the one giving short, cutoff cries as he drives into you again and again. Your skin is on fire, and you're circling your fingers helplessly around your clit—you're so aroused you can't touch it directly. As JD pulls almost all the way out and then drives deep back in again, you groan audibly. You're afraid you're going to give yourself away, but it's much too late to stop.

At that second, JD draws himself all the way out, and the waitress cries, "Please, please—" her protest cut off by a moan of ecstasy as he shifts down and drops his face between her legs. The sight of his dark head moving rhythmically between her thighs takes you to the edge, pleasure rising in sharp, frantic waves as you rotate the flat of two fingertips around your clit.

The waitress starts coming, her voice rising to a hoarse near-scream as she convulses under JD. It's a moment of pure primitive energy, and he rears up over her heaving body, plunges his cock back into her, thrusts deeply, cries out, and then collapses onto her, panting.

At the same second, you have to shove your fist in your mouth as your own orgasm rips through your body so powerfully, it's close to pain. Luckily, your muffled shout is masked by the gasps and murmurs of satisfaction from the pair on the lounger.

Your heart is thundering, and your legs are wobbling, but it's now or never, if you're to make your escape. You dart out in the direction of freedom, bending as you run. You think you hear surprised sounds behind you, but you put your head down and belt across the lawns at top speed. You can't believe what you just saw and did—it must be wedding fever combined with the full moon, you tell yourself.

You pause at the entrance to tug at your dress and catch your breath. Hopefully Steve will long since have gone to bed. All you want now is the sanctuary of your

Helena L. Paige

room—and maybe a quiet minute to replay the image of those magnificent bodies twining around each other in the candlelight—and then a good night's sleep, so that you won't have bags under your eyes at tomorrow's rehearsal dinner.

❧ Go to page 98.

a girl walks into a wedding

❧ You decide you have to get out of there

YOU'RE HOPING THAT JD and the waitress are just going to exchange free and frank views on the economy, but no such luck. Your plans for a speedy escape are dashed as he pulls her shirt off over her head. Wow, he moves fast, you think with a little stab of jealousy. You feel a forbidden rush—if you were really daring, you might step out of hiding, announce your presence, and offer to join them. Wait, where did that idea come from? You feel a little hot and bothered by your evil thoughts. You shift, and your foot knocks against one of the chairs.

The couple freezes. "What's that?" whispers the waitress, covering her breasts.

"Hello?" calls JD.

Oh lord, the embarrassment if you're caught. You hold your breath.

"See, it's nothing, just nature," he says. "Now, where was I?" And he slides a hand up under her skirt.

The waitress moans in a rather dramatic fashion.

Urgh, you think, she's a screamer. It's definitely time to get out of here.

You wait until the waitress has her eyes closed, her mouth open, and JD's head is buried in her lap, then you make a run for it. You'll never be able to look either of them in the face again, but you can't worry about that now. All you want is to get back to your room. And rinse out your eyes. Preferably with disinfectant.

Hopefully Steve will have given up the hunt and gone back to his own room by now. After the assorted dramas of the day, you're hoping for a good night's sleep so that you'll be fresh for the rehearsal dinner tomorrow night.

❧ Go to page 98.

a girl walks into a wedding

🙠 You've decided to sneak down to the bar
for a nightcap

As you head through the entrance hall, you see a couple locked in an embrace on the steps outside the front door. You recognize JD and one of the waitresses who was serving champagne at the get-together earlier. They disappear into the night, hands joined. You smother a jab of regret and slip into the bar, which is empty except for the receptionist, who looks to be closing it up for the night, and a man sitting at a table in the corner.

It's Mikey, Tom's disreputable best man. "Hey," he calls. "Join me for a drink?"

You hesitate. But while Mikey may have the morals of Charlie Sheen, he's never boring. You've probably had enough alcohol for one night, so you order an orange juice and join him.

"Why aren't you at the bachelor party?" you ask.

He shrugs. "We ended up in a pub full of ancient farmers who were all roaring drunk. Not my scene."

You hear the faint sound of Steve's voice: "Ba-a-abe!" Without hesitating, you duck under the table.

"While you're down there . . ." Mikey says.

"Shhhh!" You count backward from twenty, then stick your head out from beneath the table. "Is it all clear?"

"Yes. He's gone. What's going on?" Mikey asks.

"Don't ask," you say.

"He seems like a good guy."

"Really?"

"Sure. He's a real laugh."

Clearly Mikey is as bad at sizing people up as he is at having grown-up relationships. "Thanks for not giving me away."

"So how about doing me a favor in return?"

"What kind of favor?" You shoot him a skeptical look.

"Something fun, I promise."

He gets up. Curious, you follow him outside, your feet crunching across the gravel.

"What are we doing out here?" you ask.

"This way," he laughs. He's heading for the wedding car—an exquisite silver vintage Rolls-Royce. He opens the passenger door and waves you inside.

You pause and he gives you one of his lazy grins. He's sexy, there's no doubt about it—he saves lives, and goes rock climbing in his spare time, so he has that wiry, chiseled physique. But you know it wouldn't lead anywhere—except maybe to a highly regrettable one-night stand, and you're not that kind of girl.

Or are you?

❧ If you decide it's time to go to bed—alone,
   go to page 87.

❧ If you decide to see what Mikey has in mind,
   go to page 88.

& You've decided to go to bed

YOU CREEP ALONG THE hallway to your room, praying that Steve has given up for the night. You really are a coward. Why not just tell him you're not interested instead of sneaking around like a schoolgirl?

Nope. He's still prowling around outside your bedroom door. You tiptoe away again, cursing both him and yourself. This time, you flee outside. It's the most beautiful night; the earlier clouds have cleared, and the lawns are silver in the moonlight.

You wander down to the lake, making your way to the summerhouse that stands at the water's edge. There are chairs stacked against the walls, and a lounge chair that overlooks the lake. You stretch out on it to admire the big, round moon.

Peace at last.

& Go to page 75.

ᔥ You've decided to see what Mikey has in mind

MIKEY DRIVES THE ROLLS across the lawn and parks it under a tree next to the lake.

"What the hell are we doing?" you ask.

"Wait and see."

He gets out, opens the trunk, and removes several boxes of what appear to be shaving-cream canisters, empty tin cans, and women's underwear.

He thumps them down next to you and hands you a can of shaving cream, shaking another in his hand. "Let's go for it."

"Are you crazy? You're only supposed to trash the wedding car on the day of the wedding."

"Thought we could give it a trial run."

"Is this just an excuse to cover me in shaving cream?" you ask.

"Maybe. I like the idea of getting you all lathered up."

Before you can react, he points a can at you and sprays. You squeal, then dive into the box to arm yourself with a second can.

Five minutes later, you're both panting, giggling, and covered with foam. "This is ridiculous," you say. "I've got this stuff everywhere, even in my hair. And I'm supposed to look my best this weekend."

"No worries," says Mikey airily. "I know a way to get us both clean."

He grabs your hand and drags you toward the lake. You dig in your heels at first, but it's a glorious night, and a midnight swim might be just what you need to clear your head.

Kicking off your shoes, you both charge into the water. It feels shocking but exhilarating, and soft mud blooms between your toes as you splash each other. You launch yourself backward, kicking up sprays of water. A waterfowl scolds somewhere in the reeds.

Even in the moonlight, you can see that Mikey's eyes are riveted to your chest—the combination of clinging foam and cold water has rendered the thin fabric of your dress entirely superfluous: Every ridge on your bullet-hard nipples is clear. He floats over to you. "Is it cold or are you happy to see me?" he says, nodding at your chest.

You splash him again and paddle away, chuckling, "In your dreams." You wade into the shallows and pick your way up the sloping lawn toward the car. The night is balmy, but you're dripping wet and goose-bumped, your dress plastered to your body.

a girl walks into a wedding

You turn to watch as Mikey rises out of the water and starts moving toward you. In the silvery glow of the night, he looks like a classic sculpture of a minor god come to life. No matter how hot, he's not your type—he's not any sane woman's type—but you still can't help staring as he slowly undoes his shirt buttons and peels off the wet fabric, his rock-hard pecs so clearly defined you could chisel something with them. Perhaps it's time for a cold shower, you think, since the fresh splash of the lake doesn't seem to have cooled you down.

Mikey, now only in painted-on jeans, joins you at the car and roots around in a box. "Here," he says, pulling out a bottle of amber liquid. "Something to warm you up."

"What's this?"

"Try it."

You sniff it—it smells lethal. "You first," you say.

Mikey takes a mouthful, grimacing as he swallows it.

You take a sip. It burns as it goes down. "What is this, moonshine?" you ask.

"Mampoer. It's from South Africa. Got it on my last trip."

You take another sip, feeling its heat blossoming in your chest. It's definitely doing the trick.

He turns the car radio on. "Want to dance?"

You're about to make your excuses, when the unmistakable rhythms of a tango start up. You love the dance—it's so sexy and somehow filled with yearning at the same time. But wouldn't it be more sensible to go back to your room, get out of your wet dress, and get some sleep?

❧ If you decide to dance with Mikey, go to page 92.

❧ If you head back to your room for a good night's sleep, go to page 98.

a girl walks into a wedding

You decide to dance with Mikey

"OKAY, YOU'RE ON," YOU say. "But if I'm going to dance with you, I'll need another sip of that moonshine."

"Coming right up!" Mikey hands you the bottle, and you take a long swig, feeling it flame all the way down and flood your veins with courage.

"Right, let's see if you know what you're doing." You step closer to Mikey, laying one hand in his and curling the other around his shoulder, and you're pleasantly surprised when he takes the correct position, drawing you close, sliding his hand onto the proper part of your back and molding his body to yours.

You feel him rocking gently to the music before taking a step, drawing you into the rhythm. Then, in perfect time with the plaintive violins, you begin to move, walking together, falling into the old familiar rhythms of gliding forward, then back, then to each side.

You're both a little rusty, but Mikey's balance is good, and the lessons you took in college from an Argentine maestro come back to you, your body remembering the shapes and patterns of the dance.

"How on earth do you know how to do this?" you ask, as Mikey steers you into the typical tango cross.

"My mother was a huge tango fan," he says. "She even taught it at some stage. I'm a terrible dancer in general, but some things stuck."

For a while, you concentrate on his lead, wondering where he'll take you next, then you relax and grow bolder, trusting Mikey to steady you as you swivel your hips and shoulders, even trying out those sexy little back kicks.

He blocks your foot, you throw it back in in response. "Nice!" he says, sliding his leg between yours and hooking you into a leg wrap. You can feel the heat of his body through the wet fabric of his jeans, and as your chests press together, you might as well be naked. As you break the embrace to move backward, swinging this way and that, your nipples graze his bare skin, and you both shiver—it's the cool night, you tell yourself.

You'd forgotten how sensuous the tango is, the way the sweeping rhythms lead you into swift, bold steps, punctuated by momentary hesitations—like courtship, you remember your teacher once telling you.

You feel Mikey's breath tickling your ear and throw

caution to the wind. When he gives the signal, you bend recklessly all the way backward, your hair almost touching the ground. He steadies you with one hand, balancing you with his hips and braced thigh, then places the flat of his fingers on your breastbone and runs them slowly down to below your navel. Then he sweeps you back upright, hard against his chest, but the dizziness is too much, and you stagger, forcing him to stumble.

Mikey's hands slide lower and lower, and then his warm mouth fastens on your neck. This really isn't a good idea, but as he nips gently, you feel a shudder run through your body.

The violins continue to play their bittersweet, insistent melody, but they sound far away, and the stars in the sky are spinning gently.

"Here, I need warming up," you say. "Where did that bottle go?"

"MOMMY?" A CHILD'S VOICE jolts you awake. "I can see that lady's rude parts."

You open your eyes and see faces staring down at you. Many, many faces. Most of them wearing expressions of shock or amusement. There's Aunt Lauren (amused), Tom (shocked), Father Declan (shocked and amused), Jane's mother (shocked), and the gorgeous JD (amused). Lisa has her hand clamped over her mouth, tears of mirth running down her face. Domino are stony-faced as they attempt to shepherd their fascinated kids away, and there's Bruno and his girlfriend, trying to stifle their giggles.

Someone groans next to you.

You sit up on your elbows, feeling a lurch of nausea as you do so. Your head feels like someone's taken a jackhammer to it, and the morning light feels like razorblades against your eyeballs. Then it hits you.

You're stark naked, lying on the grass on the front lawn of the hotel. You hastily cover your breasts with your hands. You're surrounded by condoms, their jellyfish bodies scattered about. Your shoes and panties are nestled next to the empty bottle of Mampoer and several crushed cans of industrial-strength cider.

"Someone switch those damn birds off," Mikey growls. You turn to look at him. He's also naked, and someone's written "YES U CAN" on his stomach in lipstick, with an arrow pointing to his crotch. You recognize that shade of lipstick: It's yours. You blink. Is his penis really that tiny, or is the chilly morning air partly to blame?

"My head," another voice moans. You look past Mikey's prone body and see the receptionist. He's wearing your dress and a long blonde wig. What the hell did you get up to last night?

You try to piece it together. You and Mikey were dancing around the wedding car, passing the bottle of South African moonshine between you, giggling and having a great time.

The rest is a blank.

"Baaaabe." You never knew so much sorrow and

a girl walks into a wedding

disappointment could be packed into a single syllable. It's Steve, shaking his head as he gallantly pulls off his yellow T-shirt (attracting a lascivious look from Aunt Lauren), holds it by his fingertips, and tosses it to you. You pull it over your head. It's long enough to cover your nakedness, but nothing will ever be long enough to cover your shame.

A high-pitched scream, laced with hysteria, cuts through your throbbing head like a rusty hacksaw. The crowd parts and you see Cee Cee screeching and pointing at the lake.

Oh, shit.

The trunk of the wedding car is rearing out of the water, the stuffed stag's head from the bar bobbing next to it, a tiara hanging off one antler.

"Must've knocked the handbrake off at some point," Mikey says. "Gah. Feel like crap."

"What have you two *done*?" Jane hisses. "How could you?"

"Jane," you falter. "I'm really sorry—"

"You've ruined my wedding!"

Steve is still shaking his head and even Lisa is looking stern.

"Jane, I—"

"Just go," Cee Cee snaps.

Even the stag's glass eyes glint at you in judgment. You scoop up your underwear and shoes and race into the hotel, face burning. So much for worrying about Steve embarrassing you. You've managed to do that with bells, whistles, and brass knobs on—all by yourself.

You certainly can't stay in the circumstances—you'd be at risk of death by terminal blushing. So there's only one thing for it. Pack up and leave. Your disgrace is complete.

The End

a girl walks into a wedding

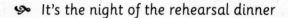

IT'S THE EVENING OF the rehearsal dinner, and as you slip into your favorite red cocktail dress and don a pair of antique jet earrings, you reflect on what a strange day it's been so far.

You're sure that Steve must have gotten the message by now (moving into your own room was a big clue, after all), and you've been steeling yourself for the inevitable "it's over" conversation—but you haven't had a chance to speak to him all day.

Straight after breakfast, Cee Cee roped you into wedding detail. You spent the morning double-checking that the team of makeup artists and hairstylists was on track for tomorrow, and helping Cee Cee count tea lights and fold napkins into fan shapes. While she did battle with the florist, you took delivery of the baskets of doves she planned to free after the ceremony (somehow you resisted the urge to contact PETA). Cee Cee kept you so busy you didn't even get a chance to talk to Jane about her cold-feet issues.

As you and Cee Cee measured the cutlery on the tables to ensure that the place settings were all precisely equidistant, Domino had wandered in. "That boyfriend of yours is a marvel," Dom told you. "He's organized a game of Wiffle ball for all the kids." You looked out of the window to see Steve gently pitching underhand to Manhattan or Paris or Tokyo, the other toddlers happily playing at his feet. As you watched, Cat and Lisa joined them, and Steve said something that made Lisa roar with laughter.

"He's been a godsend," Noe said. "It's the first time I've had a break in months. Honestly, I don't know what I would have done without him."

Then, later, as you attempted to mediate an argument between Cee Cee and the hotel chef (the chocolate on the profiteroles was the wrong shade, apparently), you caught a glimpse of Mikey, Bruno, and Steve sitting at a table in the breakfast room.

Mikey and Bruno were laughing at something Steve was saying, and then both of them bumped fists with him. It was difficult to hear exactly what was going on what with Cee Cee's shrieking and the chef's swearing, but you caught Bruno thanking Steve profusely. Strange. Downright weird, in fact.

NOW YOU CHECK YOUR makeup one last time and make your way to the room where the rehearsal dinner is being held, passing JD en route. He winks at you, and you blush and give him a small wave. At least someone had a good night last night.

Jane is looking horribly hungover, Tom only slightly better. You're introduced to Tom's father—a pilot who has the look of an action hero—and take your seat between Bruno and Steve.

Steve smiles at you sadly—he's definitely got the message. You feel a twinge of guilt. You've been behaving like a jerk. The least you could have done was say something to his face, rather than avoiding him. But the first course is being served, so you can't take him aside right this minute. According to the menu, the tiny tower of food arranged on your plate is roast endive soufflé on sage foam with zucchini batons. It's garnished with more accessories than the average wedding guest.

"Steve," you whisper as soon as the waiters have finished handing out the starters, "there's something I need to—"

You're interrupted by the sound of a knife being tinged against a glass, and Father Declan stands up. "Dear friends, we're gathered for a wonderful occasion, in which Jane and Tom will be united in happiness." He pauses and smiles at Jane, who is looking really strained. "But before we begin, I'd like to share something with you. Among our guests is someone truly selfless. Someone with a heart of gold."

At first you think that Father Declan is looking straight at you—surely helping Cee Cee fold napkins doesn't warrant this type of praise—but then you realize he's looking at Steve. "Steve here has offered to donate a sizable amount to one of my charities." The priest looks troubled for a moment. "There have been times in my life when it's been a struggle to keep the faith, but it's people like Steve and their boundless generosity who restore it. To Steve!"

Everyone beams and applauds, and Mikey claps Steve on the back.

"He also helped Bruno and me with our speeches," Mikey says. "Thanks for that, buddy. Don't know what we would have done without you."

"Hear, hear," cries Noe. Even Lisa is murmuring and nodding in approval.

Have you fallen into some sort of parallel universe?

Cee Cee gets to her feet. "Thank you, Father Declan. And thank you, Steve, for your suggestions on flower placement. I also don't know what I would have done without you! Now, I thought I'd run through tomorrow's schedule so that everyone is on the same page. At nine fifteen A.M. sharp, hair and makeup for the wedding party. Nine fifty, bride's makeup and manicure. Ten forty-five A.M., people are to make their way to the chapel . . ."

You tune her out. Could you be wrong about Steve? Everyone seems to think he's some sort of god. But . . . that terrible taste in music . . . and all that self-help nonsense!

"I can't do this!" Jane's wail cuts through your thoughts and Cee Cee's babble. She leaps up from her chair and runs from the room.

"Jane!" Your heart almost breaks at the expression on Tom's face as he races after her. You move to get up, but Bruno murmurs, "Better let them sort it out."

The other guests are all looking stunned. After a long pause, there's a general stampede for the bar. Cee Cee is pacing up and down, wringing her hands, Noe fluttering around her.

It's only then that you realize Steve is nowhere to be seen.

You go off in search of him. Eventually, following the sound of voices, you find the three of them on the back veranda, overlooking a trickling fountain and yet more roses. Tom and Jane are sitting on a bench with Steve. You hang back and eavesdrop for a few seconds.

"All that matters is that you're best friends," Steve is saying. "That's all you need in a relationship. The rest is window dressing."

Both Tom and Jane are crying. "We've got some talking to do," Jane says. "Thanks, Steve." She gives him a small, sad smile, then she and Tom walk off into the night, heads together, his arm around her shoulders.

You want to support your friend, but it's clear she and Tom need their space. You hope they work it out— seeing that expression on Tom's face as Jane fled told you everything you needed to know about their relationship. He loves her, and cold feet or not, you're sure she feels the same way.

You join Steve on the veranda. "Mind if I sit down?"

He looks at you and squares his shoulders. "I know

Helena L. Paige

what you're going to say. I'm not stupid. I know I came on too strong."

You mumble an apology for avoiding him.

"Do me a favor," he says. "Tell me—what was it that really turned you off me? We started out so well."

Where to begin? "Well, there's the calling me 'babe' thing."

He raises his hands in acknowledgment. "You're right. That was a bit much. It's what my dad used to call my mom—my parents died a few years ago—so it doesn't have the same cheesy connotation for me it does for everyone else. I guess I just got carried away. I really felt we had a connection."

Okay. You're prepared to buy that. Now for the bigger issue. "And then there's all that 'Yes U Can, Man!' stuff."

He looks surprised. "What about it?"

"Um . . . to be honest, it did put me off a bit."

He shrugs. "I guess everyone's different. I showed my DVD to Lisa, Bruno, Cat, and Father Declan, and they all found it hilarious."

Wait. "Hilarious? You *wanted* them to find it hilarious?"

"Sure. And I don't think they were pretending to find it funny. Bruno's offered to air it on one of his comedy shows."

It finally hits you. "You mean . . . it's a parody?"

Steve looks at you as if you're insane. "Of course! I've been trying to get into comedy for ages. I thought you'd appreciate it. Especially after you chose that Will Ferrell movie for our first date."

Now you're feeling really stupid. "I thought you did life coaching for corporate companies or something," you say.

He laughs. "God, no. I'm a filmmaker and an actor. Work's been a bit slow lately, so I've been making these awful training videos for corporates, and I decided to have a little fun with them. I'm lucky enough to get steady royalties for an ad I did a while back, but I can't just sit around all day—I needed a project I could really sink my teeth into."

"And the singing in the car and the terrible taste in music? Was that all part of it?"

He looks confused. At least you were on the money there.

"I think it's best if I leave now," he says. "I feel a bit like a hanger-on now that it's obviously over between us." He gets to his feet.

"Steve . . . wait," you say.

He hesitates.

What are you going to tell him? Can you get over Babe-gate and his taste in music, and give him another chance—that's if he'll have you? Or are you willing to let him be the one who got away?

If you ask Steve to stay, go to page 105.

If you decide to let him go, go to page 107.

✎ You ask Steve to stay

 "STEVE . . ." YOU BEGIN. "I've been a real idiot. I honestly thought you were some weirdo self-help guru. With the T-shirts and everything . . ."

He laughs. "I can see why that would be a bit of a turnoff."

You take a deep breath. The last thing you want is to come across as desperate, but what if you've made a huge mistake? As far as you can tell, his only real faults are poor taste in music and endearments, and those are easy enough to fix. And you definitely felt something for him on the journey here. Even the setting is on the side of romance, with the fountain tinkling quietly in the fragrant night air. Surely it's a sign that you and Steve should start afresh. "Is there any chance I can convince you to stay? It would be a shame to leave now. Everyone will be so disappointed."

"Including you?" he asks.

"Yes," you say.

He moves toward you, and you tilt your face up to him, shutting your eyes, expecting to feel his lips on yours.

Nothing happens.

"No," he says. "I'm sorry, but this isn't going to work. I can't believe you thought I was serious about that 'Yes U Can' stuff. I just can't be with someone who doesn't have a sense of humor."

He puts out a hand and shakes your unresisting paw briskly. "Good luck, and I hope we can stay friends. Say good-bye to all the others for me."

You're speechless as you watch him and his perfect behind stride away. You want to shout after him, "Of course I have a sense of humor, I'm flipping hilarious! Come back here and I'll prove I'm even funnier than . . . than . . ." But your mind has gone completely blank, so you just stay rooted to the spot.

What just happened there? Did you really manage to chase away the most suitable guy you've met in months? Unable to face rejoining the others, you decide to creep off to bed and lick your wounds. Tempting as it is to drink yourself into a coma, it looks like Jane will need you tomorrow. You'd better keep a clear head.

❧ Go to page 119.

🙠 You've decided to let Steve go

"STEVE . . ." YOU BEGIN. "I'm sorry it has to
end like this."

He shrugs. "I knew I was taking a chance coming
here. We should probably have taken it slower. Still
friends?"

"Still friends," you smile.

"Tell you what," he says. "Before I head back to
town—you want to watch my DVD? I've been looking
forward to showing it to you."

You think about it. Jane and Tom are busy working through their issues—you want to be there for your
friend, but it's obvious she needs space right now—and it
would beat returning to the rehearsal dinner and dealing
with Cee Cee, who will no doubt have a million hysterical
questions about Tom and Jane. "Sure," you say.

You follow him to the room, neither of you speaking.
He steps back to let you in first, and as your arms brush,

you feel a frisson of the original chemistry crackling in the air between you. Just good friends, you tell yourself. The last thing you need at the moment is more complications.

Steve orders you both club sandwiches from room service, sits next to you on the bed—leaving a "just good friends" gap—and hits play.

YOU HAVEN'T LAUGHED THIS much in ages—your sides are still aching. Steve has managed to parody self-help speak perfectly, Sacha Baron Cohen–style, and without making the mistake of going for all the obvious punch lines. You have to admit it's been a lot of fun.

"I can see why Bruno would want this on his show," you say. "It's fantastic."

"Thank you," Steve says, reaching over and wiping a smear of mayonnaise from the corner of your mouth. There's no mistaking the buzz of sexual tension and unfinished business between the two of you.

Next thing you know, you're leaning into his mouth and kissing him. He pulls back in surprise for a second, then presses into you, cradling your head in his hands as he kisses you back, his tongue urgent in your mouth. In all your irritation, you had forgotten how good it feels to be kissed by him. When he shifts away at last, you reach for him again, desperate for more of him, all of him.

You find yourselves kneeling on the bed, facing each other. As you kiss, you unbutton his shirt, and he pulls your dress up at the hem, but has to wait when he reaches your head because you don't want to stop kissing him for even a second. When you finally pause so he can pull the dress all the way off, you reach for his belt frantically and undo it, then whip it out of its loops and throw it across the room. His jeans follow, leaving him in boxer shorts that barely contain his now sizable erection.

Steve lays you back on the bed, places a pillow under your head, and straddles you. Then he runs his head over you, his nose tracing over your cheek and down the side of your ear, making every hair on your body stand on end. He tracks down your neck and chest, his nose still barely grazing you.

"Touch me," you beg. He shakes his head, his hair stroking your collarbone, a maddening tease.

He unclips your bra in the front, releasing your breasts, and you can feel his warm breath on your nipple, but he still doesn't touch you—instead he keeps roaming your body with the tip of his nose and his eyelashes and the fringe of his hair, and you think you might die if he doesn't touch you soon.

So you drag him down onto the bed and roll over onto him, sitting astride him, feeling his hard cock pressing against you. You rotate your hips, savoring the pressure against your pussy. He holds your hip with one hand, reaching for your breast with the other, and you arch your back as he massages it between his fingers, the bud of your nipple instantly hard between his fingers.

He stops briefly to reach across the bed for his toiletry bag, pulling out a condom and something else in plastic packaging. He puts the condom on the bedside table, and sits up with you still straddling his lap, then opens his hand to reveal what he's holding.

"What is it?" you ask.

"It's a vibrator," he says, tearing the packaging open. It's not like any one you've ever seen before. It's pink and made out of silicone, and it fits neatly in his palm. It's got a circular loop, with a bullet-shaped nugget at the top. In fact, it looks like a ring you might wear on your finger, only bigger.

"Here, feel," he says, dropping it into your open hand. Then he presses on the side of the bullet, and it comes alive, vibrating against your skin. He presses it a second time, and the vibrating ramps up so that the little toy is bouncing in your palm.

🖎 If you want to try out the toy, go to page 111.

🖎 If you'd rather keep things simple, go to page 114.

❧ You want to try out the toy

YOU DON'T KNOW WHAT Steve's going to do with his vibrating toy, but you can't wait to find out. He presses the bullet again and it stills itself. Then he pushes you gently back onto the giant bed, places his arms on either side of your head, and dips down to kiss you again. You surrender yourself to his mouth for what feels like hours. Then he reaches for the condom and takes it out of its wrapper. You help him slip it over his rigid cock.

Next, he takes the small toy and buzzes it back to life again, sending a thrill of curiosity racing down your spine. He slips the expanding silicone ring over the tip of his cock and rolls it all the way down over the condom, making sure that the vibrating bullet is on the top side of his penis.

Kneeling on the bed, he parts your legs, and you feel the tip of his cock nudging against your pussy, the slight sensation of the tremors from the base of his cock teasing you. He guides the head up and down your slit, not entering you yet. Then he takes one of your nipples in his mouth, his hot tongue lapping at the hard nub of it. You buck your hips, eager to get him to slip inside you, and to your relief, he does.

The farther inside you he pushes, the more intensely you can feel the toy's vibrations, until he's all the way into you, and you can finally feel the full effect of the small bullet vibrating at speed right up against your clit. He pushes your knee up against your chest so he can penetrate even deeper. Then he pulls almost completely out of you, but only momentarily, before thrusting back inside you so that the bullet rubs up against your clit once more. The buzzing against your clit and the walls of your pussy send your whole body into a frenzy.

You tilt your head back into the softness of the duvet and hold on to his shoulders, urging him on, harder, faster, the vibrations coursing through the whole of your lower body. The pleasure builds up in you with every thrust, first rising, then surging, the pressure is almost unbearable until you finally come, shouting out so loudly the entire hotel can probably hear you.

Steve rolls onto his back beside you, and once you've recovered a little, you straddle him, riding him reverse cowboy–style this time, so that he can slip his cock effortlessly back inside you. And because you're facing away from him, the bullet of the vibrator is no longer focused on your clit, which is swollen and sensitive from your monster orgasm, but is concentrated on the back wall of your pussy, sending delicious volts through a part of you that you're not sure has been stimulated like this before.

You grip his thighs and rotate your hips as you push back against each of his thrusts, relishing the sound of the bullet buzzing and his skin slapping against yours. You can't believe it, but the intensity is rising inside you once again as he holds on to your bottom, kneading at it, until you finally come a second time, this time squeezing your eyes tight and curling your toes, unable to tell which of your two orgasms was more powerful.

Steve ramps up to a frenetic pace, going from long deep thrusts to short hard ones, groaning as you push back and down on his cock, clamping your pussy and thigh muscles tightly around him, still feeling the vibrations of the small toy all along the length of his cock. You realize that as much as you can feel every vibration along the length of your pussy, he must be able to feel it all through his shaft, too. He squeezes your hips as he comes with a grunt and a couple of shudders.

You spread out beside him, breathless and completely spent. Every inch of you is tingling. The buzzing stops as Steve slips the ring off his cock, turns it off, and drops it on the bed. Between his kisses, that marvelous little pink toy, and his incredibly hard cock, that was easily the best sex of your life.

∾ Go to page 117.

a girl walks into a wedding

❧ **You want to have sex with Steve without the toy**

YOU PROD THE VIBRATING ring in Steve's palm, then wrap an arm around his neck—never mind his toy, you want more of those incredible kisses. As your tongues meet, you feel the hard press of his erection against your leg, and you run your fingers down his back.

When you finally come up for air, you look into his eyes, then trail your hand over his groin, feeling him respond immediately under the fabric. "You know what?" Your voice comes out a growl. "I don't think we're going to need any help." You snatch the vibrating bullet and toss it aside, then slip your thumb through the gap in his shorts, running it up the side and over the top of his cock as he groans in pleasure.

Steve pushes you back on the bed and slips your panties off in one move. Then it's his turn as you help him get rid of his underwear, ecstatic to find his long, hard cock pulsing.

You seize handfuls of the duvet underneath you as he runs two fingers up and down from your cunt to your clit, making you arch, your moans no longer quiet. And then you gasp as his mouth envelops your clit, and his fingers push inside you, opening you up. You want to scream every time his tongue hits your clit. And then he's doing something different with his tongue, something you've never experienced before, twisting it around and around as he pushes in and out of your pussy like a drill, first in one direction and then in the other, and every nerve in your body sings.

When you're no longer able to bear it, you pull him up to you and roll around on the bed kissing, your legs wrapped around each other, until you tumble off the edge of the bed together, your fall cushioned by the king-size coverlet you'd kicked to the floor earlier. And then you go back to kissing on the floor, laughing into each other's mouths.

You wrap your palm around his cock and rub up and down as his fingers find your clit, and both your hands move in time together.

"Fuck me now," you pant, worried that you might come before he even gets inside you, then you both laugh again as he reaches up and fumbles around for the condom he left on the bedside table.

Eventually he snags it, tears the packaging open, then rolls the condom onto his cock in one smooth movement. You lie back on the floor in the soft folds of the silken coverlet as he positions himself between your legs and enters you slowly, your eyes locked. He rocks against you, and then ramps up his speed until he's pounding into you in time with your moans.

"I want to come with you," he breathes, and you lift your hips to match his thrusts, urging him harder, faster, begging for more, both of you riding the same wave of extreme pleasure until it breaks over you, and you come at the exact same time, shouting out together, your fingers digging into each other's skin, eyes squeezed tight in the moment of the explosion. You feel salt on your tongue, and you don't know if it's sweat or tears, or his or yours.

Steve collapses next to you and you sprawl beside him, your chest heaving, every inch of your body tingling. As far as sex goes, that was right up there with the best you've ever had.

❧ Go to page 117.

Helena L. Paige

❧ You've just had mind-blowing sex with Steve

"ARE YOU THINKING WHAT I'm thinking?"
you say to Steve, when you finally get your wits back.

He nods. "Yeah. Sorry, that was awful, wasn't it? I
guess I was wrong. Clearly we're not compatible after all."

You're stunned. Surely he must be joking? "Are you
being serious?"

"You must have felt it, too, right? That lack of connection. What were we thinking? This could never work."

"Right . . . felt it, too . . . lack of connection . . . never
work . . ." you parrot. The only thing you felt was an as-
tonishingly good orgasm bonanza.

"I guess sometimes it's just not meant to be." He
smiles wryly. "But at least we gave it a shot, and now we
have closure, right?" He pats you platonically on the arm.
Then he looks at his watch. "If I leave now, I can get back
to town before it's too late."

You watch speechless from your nest of bedding as he pulls on his clothes and packs up his DVDs.

"Thanks for inviting me, and please say bye to everyone from me. Oh, and tell Father Declan I'll be in touch about sponsoring that school in Somalia." He kisses you chastely on top of your head. "It's a shame things didn't work out for us," he says before slipping out the door.

You can't believe it. You just let a funny, smart, super-hot sex god slip between your fingers. You drum your heels and think about raiding the minibar. But the last thing you need tomorrow is a hangover and puffy eyes.

Your hideous bridesmaid dress mocks you from its hanger on the wardrobe. You wonder if Jane and Tom have ironed things out. Your best friend will need you to be there for her either way, and being a self-pitying mess won't help anyone.

Wait, it looks like Steve didn't pack everything. Your eye catches the vibrating cock ring, and you reach for it to examine more closely. At least he left you a little something to remember him by. And if you're going to be a single girl this weekend, you might as well be a single girl with a vibrator!

๛ Go to page 119.

Helena S. Paige

❧ It's the morning of the wedding

YOU SIP YOUR MORNING coffee. Everyone keeps asking you where Steve is, and you feel like throttling them all. You've made up an excuse about him having to jet off to an emergency comedy conference, but no one's buying it. Even worse is that tablecloth dress lurking in your room. The last thing you feel like doing is putting the damn thing on, but you're going to have to woman-up and take one for the team.

Cee Cee bustles into the breakfast room, giant curlers haloing her head. "Why aren't you in your dress?" she barks at you. "And where is Jane? The manicurist is here. I hope she's worked out all her issues."

You mumble something about not having seen Jane yet this morning, and let Cee Cee shepherd you into the room where a team of makeup artists and hairdressers are waiting, brandishing mascara wands and curling irons. Aunt Lauren and Noe are already being primped and curled.

The makeup artist flutters around you, piling on the foundation. You glance in the mirror. Fantastic. You look like a cast member of *RuPaul's Drag Race*.

Oh well. There's no chance of getting lucky anyway. Steve has gone, JD has hooked up with someone else, and you'd need to get blind drunk to even consider Mikey. You sigh. It's time to crowbar yourself into the bridesmaid dress.

The door opens and Jane walks in. She's dressed in jeans and a T-shirt.

"Finally!" Cee Cee says.

"I have something to tell you all," Jane announces.

☙ If Jane tells you the wedding is on, go to page 121.

☙ If Jane tells you the wedding is off, go to page 145.

❧ The wedding is on

YOUR CHEST FEELS TIGHT, but you're not sure if this is because you're constricted by the Hell Dress or because you're all choked up. Jane, radiant with happiness, looks more beautiful than you could possibly have imagined, and you feel weepy with emotion as she reaches for Tom's hand at the front of the chapel.

You managed to snatch a few minutes to talk to her alone after she had marched into the dressing room and announced the wedding would be going ahead as planned, and she assured you she felt good about her decision.

"Tom and I are best friends," she said. "Steve was right. It is the only thing that matters in the end."

You're genuinely happy for her. After the weekend you've had, you can understand the attraction of spending the rest of your life with someone you trust and know inside out.

Father Declan clears his throat. "If anyone knows any reason why these two should not be joined in holy matrimony, speak now, or forever hold your peace."

The hush is broken by a sound. A ripping, popping sound.

Hang on . . . Why does your chest suddenly feel all breezy? You look down to see that your bridesmaid dress has split from the neckline to the waist.

The intense silence is broken by a squeal of horror from Cee Cee. Father Declan is gulping. You do your best to cover yourself with your hands, which is a little tricky given that you're juggling both your bouquet and Jane's. Mikey is silently clapping, Tom's dad is grinning broadly, and Lisa is openly hooting.

Then you feel something being draped over your shoulders. Bruno relieves you of the bouquets so you can slip your arms into his jacket.

You mutter "Thanks," and mouth "Sorry" at Jane, who mouths back "Classic."

Bruno catches your eye and whispers, "Don't worry."

You give him a grateful look. Who would have thought that your old enemy would be the one to help you out?

Father Declan, now the color of a tomato, stumbles on with the ceremony, and everyone claps and cheers as he declares that Tom and Jane are now husband and wife. A string quartet strikes up, and you slink down the aisle behind the happy couple, trying to pretend that a man's jacket over a buttonless bodice and a lot of skin is what all the best bridesmaids are wearing this season.

Helena L. Paige

"Way to make a tit of yourself," Lisa says, sidling up next to you.

"Ha, ha. I wasn't expecting to hear that at *all*."

She nudges you. "Lighten up! This is one wedding no one will ever forget."

"Yeah. I'll be *that* woman."

"The bridesmaid who made a boob."

You sigh. "No one can say I didn't have the breast intentions for the day, though."

Lisa rolls her eyes, and you both giggle. Mikey shoots you a lascivious glance, and Lisa gives him the finger.

As Jane and Tom leave the chapel, Cee Cee and a couple of the staff release the long-suffering white doves from their baskets. But not even the spectacle of several of them crapping on Cee Cee's upswept hairdo can entirely blunt your humiliation.

Amid cheers, Jane throws the bouquet. Lisa catches it, yelps in dismay, and immediately throws it to Aunt Lauren, who in turn chucks it away as if it's on fire. Cat ends up catching it, and you surprise yourself by feeling a brief pang of regret.

You try to make a dash for your room before heading to the reception, so you can change out of your torn dress, but Cee Cee intercepts you.

"You can't get changed!" she orders. "You'll clash with the flower girls and ruin the photographs. Just hold your bouquet in front of you."

It takes every bit of your resolve not to tell Cee Cee to shove the bouquet where the sun don't shine, but a screaming catfight is the last thing Jane needs today.

You compromise by wearing Bruno's jacket until the very last moment, and somehow get through the photographs without too much embarrassment.

As you walk into the room where the reception's being held, you try to console yourself. It's not as if the wedding weekend could get any worse, could it?

Yep. It could. The tablecloths and napkins really do match your ruined dress.

THE SPEECHES ARE OVER, and you slump in your chair, knocking back your third glass of champagne. You've been seated at the kids' table—a sly bit of name-card shuffling on the part of Domino, who are happily getting drunk with Mikey and a few of Tom's friends.

Tom's dad stands up, gives you a hopeful smile, and starts weaving his way toward your table. He's attractive, with those rugged looks, but you hope he isn't coming over to chat you up—with the whole dress debacle, you're just not in the mood for small talk. One of the Domino children (Manhattan? Montreal? Mogadishu?) announces that she wants to go for a wee-wee.

"Do you need me to come with you?" you ask.

"I'm not a baby," she says haughtily. Great. Even the kids are treating you like an idiot.

Tom's dad is waylaid by Aunt Lauren, and you heave a sigh of relief.

The little girl races back to the table. "Two ladies kissing!" she squeals. "I saw two ladies kissing! One had pink hair."

You stare. She can only mean Lisa.

"Now look here, Moscow or Maputo or whatever your name is," you snap. "It's very bad to make up stories."

"But I did see them kissing!" Her voice rises like a siren. "And they were squeezing each other's chests."

Oh, shit. You dart out into the hall just in time to see Cat and Lisa emerging from one of the alcoves.

"Lisa!" you hiss.

Lisa turns, catches your eye, and smiles radiantly. Cat murmurs something to her, gives you an unreadable look, and strolls off in the direction of the rooms.

"What are you *doing?*" you ask.

"What can I say? For the first time in my life I've met someone who is both nice and not boring."

"But . . . Cat has a boyfriend." Lisa may be a lot of things, but she's not a cheater—you've never known her to sneak around behind someone's back.

"What's going on?" a child's voice says behind you. "Are *you* going to kiss the lady, too?"

"I'll tell you about it later," Lisa says to you, without the faintest trace of guilt. She hurries after Cat.

You slink back to the reception and help the tots cut their wild-mushroom-and-apricot-stuffed chicken breasts into tiny pieces, in the vain hope that they might actually eat the stuff. But they make the judges on *Master Chef* look like teddy bears. They've already declared the asparagus and truffle soup with tempura watercress garnish to be "slimy," and secretly you agree. Even the politest member of the Domino clan—Yodabell the rat,

a girl walks into a wedding

safely ensconced in his cage under the table—turned up his nose at it.

Someone touches your shoulder, and you look up to see Bruno. "Have you seen Cat?" he asks.

Your face burns. "Um. Let's see. Have I seen Cat? Why?" It's the best you can do.

"She's supposed to decorate the bridal suite, but she's disappeared. Cee Cee's roped me into doing it instead, but it's not really my thing. I don't suppose you feel like helping me, do you?"

Hmm. It would give you an excuse to escape the reception. You're going to bite the next person who makes a boob joke or leers, plus it will get you away from the children's table. But after what you've just witnessed, how awkward is it going to be spending time alone with Bruno?

"Come on," he says. "I promise to have you back in time for the first dance."

You can't really say no. With a twinge of glee, you mention to Domino that you'll no longer be acting as their unpaid babysitter and slip out of the room with Bruno.

Cee Cee has left a basket of rose petals and a bottle of champagne in a cooler outside the bridal suite. Part of you registers the magnificence of the room—which has a four-poster bed that could sleep an entire family, a glittering crystal chandelier, and acres of pearl silk draped everywhere—as you desultorily start scattering petals around the room.

"Hey, what's the matter?" Bruno asks. "This is a wedding, not a funeral."

"I'm fine," you lie.

"C'mon, Stinky. There's something on your mind."

Dammit. You curse Lisa for putting you in this position. Bruno saved you back at the wedding, after all. You may have a history of burning each other's hair and destroying each other's prized property, but no one deserves to be cheated on, do they?

What are you going to do?

ȣ If you tell Bruno about Lisa and Cat, go to page 128.

ȣ If you decide to keep it to yourself, go to page 140.

a girl walks into a wedding

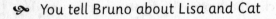

๑ You tell Bruno about Lisa and Cat

"BRUNO . . . I DON'T know how to tell you this, but . . ." Why is being honest so hard?

"Spit it out, for fuck's sake."

"Um . . . it's Cat. She and Lisa . . . look, there's no easy way to say this, but . . ."

"What? Are you trying to tell me that they've hooked up?"

"You know?"

"Of course."

"But she's your girlfriend."

"No, she's not!" He starts to laugh. "Hadn't you realized that Cat's gay? We're just really good friends."

"Oh."

"If I had come to this wedding alone, I would've never heard the end of it from my mother. 'Why are you still single? When are you going to meet a nice girl?' You know what my mom's like: She's a stuck record when it comes to weddings and grandchildren. I love her, but it's exhausting. So Cat was nice enough to volunteer to come with me to run interference."

"Oh." It's all you seem capable of saying.

"Mom can't seem to understand that I don't want to be with just anyone. I'm waiting for a certain someone to finally . . . get it."

"Get it?" you whisper.

"Yes, this girl I've known for a really long time needs to get how much I really liked her when we were kids." His voice is a little husky. "How much I think I still like her." He picks the carnation out of the lapel of his jacket—the jacket you're still wearing.

"Thanks, by the way . . ." you say, your voice coming out as a squeak, your mind racing almost as fast as your heart has started hammering. "For helping me out the way you did, during the wedding."

"Pleasure. Only . . . it's getting a little chilly." Bruno takes the lapels of his jacket and tugs at them gently, pulling you toward him. He smells of aftershave, and you have to curb the urge to bury your face in his neck. You can just feel the outline of his fingers pressed against your chest where he's clutching the lapels.

"It is?" you say. "Funny, because I'm beginning to feel rather warm."

"Then you won't mind giving me back my jacket," Bruno says. He trails a finger from just under your chin, down your neck, very slowly and tentatively down your chest to where your cleavage is framed by the V of the jacket, and down, down, down, slipping open each jacket button effortlessly as he gets to it. His finger is so soft on your skin that your breath catches.

"You want it back right now?" you whisper.

He holds your eyes. "Right this second."

❧ To take things further with Bruno, go to page 131.

❧ To head back to the reception, go to page 143.

❧ You take things further with Bruno

YOUR THROAT GOES TIGHT. You're suddenly unable to look each other in the eye. It's strange, feeling shy with someone you've known your entire life.

"Bruno—"

"Maybe—"

You both speak at once. Then he shakes his head. "Nah, forget it. Look, I'll see you back at the reception, okay?"

"Aren't you forgetting something?"

As he turns back to you, you shrug his jacket off your shoulders, and stand with your breasts exposed to him, your nipples hardening as he stares at you, his throat moving.

Then he moves toward you, you take half a step forward, and you're holding each other, laughing and panting, and then not laughing anymore as your faces nudge closer together, and then—tentatively, you don't want to break this new spell—you touch his lips with yours. And then his mouth opens, and your tongues touch, still hesitantly—and it doesn't feel weird, it feels disconcertingly right and familiar and warm, and then you're devouring each other, and his hands are sliding up over your shoulders and fighting the damn dress.

You turn around, and he wrenches the zipper open with sheer brute force. It feels so good to be free of the stiff fabric, and even better when Bruno steps up close behind you, lifts your hair away from your neck, then kisses it, nipping just a little, sliding his mouth down the sweep of your neck and onto the length of your shoulder, nibbling and kissing his way along to the top of your arm.

You're shivering, part desire and part anticipation, and as he repeats the treatment for the other side of your neck, you feel his erection pressing against you even through the voluminous skirt of the dress. God, who knew he was so well endowed?

You turn in the circle of his arms. "Get this stupid thing off me," you beg. Even with two of you helping, the dress puts up a fight, and as you step out of it, wobbling on your heels, you lose your balance, and tumble sideways onto the soft carpet, crushing the scattered petals. Bruno sinks down with you, and then you're lying in each other's arms, you just in your underwear and heels.

You lock eyes with each other: You know this is the point of no return. Bruno places a warm and slightly trembling hand low on your belly—then he slides one

fingertip just below the elastic of your panties, still holding your eyes.

"Yes," you breathe. "Yes, please." And you slip your
hands down and push off the scrap of lace and cotton,
and he helps, rolling it down until you're naked.

"Your turn," you say, as you attack his shirt and tie.
You curse as you start on his buttons, but he simply pulls
the entire shirt off over his head. Shoes, socks, trousers,
and finally shorts fly to corners of the room, and then
the full length of his naked body, its different textures
and contours, presses against yours.

He looks self-conscious when you draw back a little
to look at him, but you like the slight chunkiness of his
torso, the hair on his chest, the solidity of his hips. His
skin is soft to the touch, and he has the most magnificent cock: dark, thick, and swollen. You reach for it, and
he gives a strangled groan of pleasure as your fingers
fold around it and squeeze.

Then you lean forward and lick first one of his small
dark nipples, then the other. He hums with pleasure
and frustration, and when you apply your teeth, he
arches his back and his cock jumps in your hand.

"Careful, tiger, or this show will be over too soon,"
he gasps. He rolls you flat onto your back and places his
hands on either side of your shoulders, smiling down
at you, and you think, My god, it's Bruno, *Bruno* after
all these years, and then he kisses you again, deeply, his
tongue slanting against yours.

His hand slides up between your thighs, and you
open yourself up to him, sighing at the first brush of his

fingers against the folds of your cunt, and then the feel of his hand parting your lips.

"You're so wet," he murmurs. "Can I see?"

You blush, but the intimate request brings a fresh wave of heat flooding through your pelvis.

"Okay," you whisper, opening your legs so that he can kneel between them. He nudges gently at your thighs, and you pull up your knees and spread yourself for him.

You'd never usually expose yourself like this the first time, but you feel safe with Bruno, with the comfort of long familiarity, but all the surprise that comes with the heat flaring between you.

You feel him spreading your pussy lips open, his fingers sliding in the slick moisture. Then there's his warm breath on your pussy. You moan as his tongue slides slowly between your lips, pressing against the opening and then up, slowly, maddeningly, toward your clit, at the same time as he slides a finger into your cunt, crooking it slightly, making you arch.

You realize with delight, as you drown in the double sensation of his tongue lapping at your clit and his fingers sliding up and into you, that you're very close to coming, and he senses it, too, because he shifts up to lie next to you, his hand still between your thighs. But before you have time to regret the loss of his mouth, his thumb takes its place on your clit, rotating in tiny circles as his fingers continue to slide in and out of your soaking pussy.

The double sensation, intense pleasure radiating

Helena L. Paige

from both inside and out, sends you helplessly over the edge. Bruno slides an arm under your neck just in time to brace you as your orgasm cracks through your body, your body convulsing until you're dizzy. A sense of drifting takes hold as you flop like a rag doll, satiated.

Eventually you open your eyes to find Bruno's only an inch away. "I take it you weren't faking?" he smiles.

"If I was a cat, I would be purring right now. Wait, what about you?"

"No condom, and I don't want to break the mood by going and begging Mikey for some."

You giggle. "That would be a downer all right. But I do have a free hand." You reach for that amazing cock for the second time. "I know it's incredibly teenage, but why don't we make a sandwich?" you say, hooking a leg over his hip and trapping his erection between your heated bodies.

At that moment, the door flies open, and you hear Cee Cee's unmistakable voice: "What on earth is taking you so long?"

There's a pause as she takes in the sight of the two of you sprawled naked on the floor. "Oh, for Pete's sake!" she yells, charging into the bedroom and grabbing the half-empty basket of rose petals. "Do I have to do everything myself?"

THE PAIR OF YOU stumble giggling along the hallway, approximately dressed, but still fumbling with buttons and zippers. "I haven't seen Cee Cee that mad

a girl walks into a wedding

135

since I painted a moustache on her Bridal Barbie," pants Bruno.

"Talk about Cee Cee *interruptus*," you say.

"I'm in a desperate plight here," Bruno admits. "I can hardly walk upright."

"I hate to be a killjoy, but it is your sister's wedding reception. And I am her bridesmaid."

"And I hate to admit it, but you're right. Let's go and join the others—on two conditions. That you dance with me so that I know I didn't just dream this. And that later, we have a very private dance of our own."

"Deal," you say, pressing a kiss on his mouth. Although, you think, like all sensible, grown-up women, you do have an emergency condom stashed in your room—and you're deeply tempted to explore his body a little more. Would it be so very wrong to drag him off for a quickie? Or would you rather go back to the reception, biding your time until a little later?

❧ If you drag Bruno off for a quickie, go to page 137.

❧ If you go back to the reception, go to page 143.

❧ You've gone for a quickie with Bruno

You shove the bedroom door closed behind you with a foot as you strip Bruno of his clothes for the second time that evening. He's equally quick to help you out of yours, and this time there's no trace of shyness as you stare at each other's nakedness.

Then you're kissing again, tongues slanting into each other's mouths, laughing breathlessly, and Bruno walks you backward to the bed, and you collapse onto it. He's lying half over you, kissing you as if he can't get enough, and you run your hands down the length of his spine and boldly press your fingers into his buttocks.

"Who would have thought you'd grab me in the end?" he laughs in your ear, and you punish him by pinching his bottom and nipping his shoulder. Then you roll him over—you really want to take a closer look at his imposing cock.

You straddle him, kiss him slowly and thoroughly one

more time, then say, "Heading south. New continents to explore," before wriggling slowly down the length of his torso. You take your time positioning yourself before blowing softly up and down the length of his cock as he twitches and groans.

You follow up that move with the most delicate and catlike of licks, just flicking your tongue across the heated, fine-textured skin of his penis. At the same time, you nudge one hand up between his thighs to cup his balls, massaging slowly and softly. Then, taking your time, you fold your lips around just the head of his cock, in a puckered kiss, dabbling your tongue in the slit at the top.

Bruno is writhing now, his hands reaching for your breasts, cupping them as you take another inch into your mouth, sucking more strongly now, turning your head slightly from side to side so that he can feel the softness of your inner cheeks.

"Oh god," he gasps, "I'm so close, can we slow down?"

You reluctantly let his cock slip from your mouth, but keep gently squeezing his balls.

"That was fantastic," Bruno murmurs. "You're fantastic." He kneads very gently at your breasts, and you take the hint, and nestle his erection between them. The cashmere softness of his skin feels incredible, as does the pulsing heat. He presses your breasts together, capturing his cock between them, making small thrusts with his hips, and you catch the rhythm, and start to move your torso, enjoying the sensation of his shaft sliding up and down your cleavage.

Bruno's breath starts to come in short pants, and you draw away slightly, but it's too late—he gives a strangled shout and comes in a series of spasms.

You feel like Wonder Woman as you hand him tissues from the box on the bedside table and snuggle up next to him.

"I think that was a compliment you just paid me," you say as his breathing slowly returns to normal.

"It most certainly was," says Bruno, turning his head to brush your temple with his mouth.

You tickle the hair on his chest lazily. "And I have more good news. There's an emergency condom in my toiletry bag."

"This just keeps getting better! But perhaps we should save that for after the reception, then we'll have all night for that slow . . . dance you promised me."

"You're on."

❧ Go to page 143.

a girl walks into a wedding

You keep it to yourself

"COME ON, SPIT IT out," Bruno says. "How bad can it be?"

"Bad," you say. "Really, really bad." You sag onto the bed, and Bruno sits next to you.

"Okay . . . how about this? If I tell you a secret, will you tell me what's on your mind?"

"No."

He laughs. "I'm going to tell you anyway. Did you know that I've had a crush on you for years?"

You almost fall off the bed in shock. "But you burnt my hair! You spent an entire summer trying to cover me in cow shit."

"Don't you know anything? That's how eleven-year-old boys show affection. And then I liked you all through high school and college, but you were always going out with the cool guys, and I was just your best friend's fat, nerdy brother."

You're completely thrown. But what about his girlfriend? His soon-to-be ex-girlfriend, if Lisa gets her way.

"Did you really have no idea?" he asks.

"Cow shit didn't do it for me, I have to be honest," you say.

"So what does do it for you?" His voice catches a little. He reaches over and curls a twist of your hair around his fingers.

"What about Cat?" you ask. Repeating the mantra to yourself: I will not tell him about Cat and Lisa, I will not tell him about Cat and Lisa . . .

"What about her?"

"She's your girlfriend!"

Bruno stares at you, then starts to laugh. "Where did you get that idea? Cat is my best friend. And she happens to be gay. She offered to come to stop my mother from driving me insane. 'Bruno, when are you going to meet a nice girl? Bruno, why are you still single? Bruno, when are you going to get married and give me grandchildren?' She drives me absolutely berserk. And I can hardly tell her that maybe I'm single because I'm crazy enough to wonder about someone who still sees me as an annoying eleven-year-old boy."

"Oh."

"And besides, haven't you noticed that Cat's got the hots for your friend Lisa? They've been all over each other since the second they laid eyes on each other. I mean, you'd have to be blind not to have seen it."

That would be you, all right. Blind. Just look at how you got your wires crossed with Steve. Although come

to think of it, you haven't given him a thought all day. And now this . . .

You grin sheepishly. "That was the secret I was scared to tell you. I saw them together, and I didn't know what to do or say."

Bruno stands up, smiles, and holds out a hand. "Come on, why don't you go and get out of that dress before someone puts a vase and a place setting on you? Then we can get back to the party. Maybe you'll even consider dancing with me."

You nod, feeling your pulse speed up. When did he become so incredibly nice?

✎ Go to page 143.

Helena L. Paige

❧ You go back to the reception

 DIVERSIONS OVER FOR NOW, you quickly slip into another dress—a sleek black number with a demurely high neckline, but a beautifully plunging back. You touch up your makeup hastily, noticing how flushed your cheeks are.

Back at the reception, Tom and Jane are swaying together on the dance floor. Bruno is waiting for you next to the bridal table, and his face lights up when he sees you.

"Shall we?" he says, as a slow number starts. You nod, and he folds you into his arms.

Aunt Lauren has Mikey in her clutches—or the other way around (either way, both look like the cat that ate the canary), Domino are slow dancing, a batch of toddlers clinging to their legs, and Cee Cee is gripping Tom's dad with a bit too much enthusiasm.

Jane's eyes widen as she catches sight of you and Bruno, then she breaks out in a huge smile. "I can't be-

lieve it—I thought you two would never get together!"
Tom spins her around and she twirls away, laughing.

Bruno chuckles against your hair. "I guess this means I won't be calling you Stinky anymore."

"Oh, I dunno. I'm starting to feel quite kindly toward those cow pies," you say. You both snort with laughter and bump noses.

"I might even consider overlooking your cruel and unreasonable treatment of my G.I. Joe figures."

"Bruno. Shut up and kiss me."

The End

Helena S. Paige

✑ Jane tells you the wedding is off

"THE WEDDING IS OFF," Jane announces.

Cee Cee screams. She actually screams. Even the un-shockable Aunt Lauren looks flummoxed.

You throw your arms around Jane. "I'm so sorry! Are you sure this is what you want?"

Jane smiles. "Come with me, everyone."

Cee Cee is hyperventilating and has to be given a brown paper bag to breathe into. You all follow Jane outside to find Tom standing next to the wedding car, looking relaxed and happier than you've ever seen him, the words "NOT MARRIED" soaped on the rear window.

"So you're staying together?" you ask her.

She nods, and you go limp with relief.

Even an inch of foundation can't hide Cee Cee's sickly pallor. She finally finds her voice. "But . . . but . . . all my hard work! The flowers! The menu—I spent months planning it. The doves—do you have any idea how difficult it is to get hold of white doves during wedding season now that PETA is on the prowl? And . . . and the individual candleholders in the shape of angels I got from Bali! How could you *do* this to me?"

Jane holds firm. "No offense, Cee Cee. I really appreciate all the work you've put into this, but this kind of thing . . . it isn't me. And it isn't Tom, either." Jane pauses. "But the honeymoon's all paid for, so we thought why not take advantage of it?"

Cee Cee gabbles something about gold-encrusted tea lights and dissolves into tears.

"Cee Cee, try to understand. This is what we truly want," Jane says. She blows kisses at everyone and climbs gleefully into the car.

The rest of the guests—most of whom are already dressed in all their wedding finery—gather in the driveway to wave them off. Jane's mother sobs on her husband's shoulder.

Tom toots the horn, then revs the engine, kicking up gravel.

Once they're out of sight, there is a long moment of silence. Then Mikey says, "We've got food, we've got booze, and we've got tunes. Seems a shame to let it all go to waste."

Cee Cee gives a howl and runs off toward the lake, stumbling as her heels catch in the grass.

"What do you say?" Mikey turns to you. "Shall we get this party started?"

❧ If you decide to join Mikey and party the night away, go to page 148.

❧ If you decide to go after Cee Cee, go to page 156.

❧ You decided to join Mikey and party the night away

OUCH.

You open your eyes slowly, wincing as the morning sunlight slants through the windows. Your head feels like it's full of bees, and you'd kill for a glass of water right now.

Hang on . . . This room doesn't look familiar. It's far larger than yours, and judging by the vases of lilies everywhere and the rose petals scattered and crushed into the carpet, you can only be in one place—the bridal suite. And you're lying on the bridal bed, next to a mountain of pillows and duvets.

What are you doing in here? And more important, what did you get up to last night? You remember having a drink with Mikey at the bar, where you were joined by Father Declan, Cee Cee, Bruno, Lisa, and quite a few of the other guests. Mikey brought out a bottle of South

African liquor he'd collected on his latest trip, and you all had a shot or two of that.

You have a hazy recollection of slow dancing to "Careless Whisper" with Lisa and Cat, and then doing the cancan with a gaggle of guests—including Father Declan, Mikey, Bruno, Aunt Lauren, and JD.

That's all you've got.

You run your hands through your hair, which is knotted and smells like apricot liqueur, wincing as a strand catches on something. You hold your left hand to your face, squinting gingerly at it.

Oh, *shit*.

There's a gold band on your ring finger. Jane's wedding ring. Why do you now have a shadowy memory of giggling and saying "I do"?

You flinch as you hear the toilet flush. You hold your breath, waiting to see who will emerge from the bathroom.

🌣 If it's Mikey, go to page 150.

🌣 If it's Bruno, go to page 153.

❧ It's Mikey

 THE DOOR OPENS AND Mikey steps into the room, naked except for what appears to be a pair of women's underwear.

Oh god. Oh no. You've drunkenly married the worst womanizer on the planet. A man who makes Tiger Woods look like a Tibetan monk. A man who is wearing women's underwear. And judging by the color—bright pink—it isn't even yours.

"Morning," he says, riffling a hand through his hair. "Any chance you could order me a gallon of coffee from room service?"

You feel your mouth dropping open.

"Mikey?" a woman's voice calls from the bathroom. Aunt Lauren weaves out, wearing a yellow T-shirt and nothing else.

"Morning, dear," she says to you matter-of-factly, stretching and yawning as if this is the most natural situation in the world. She glances at Mikey's underwear. "Naughty boy. I was looking for those!"

You look from Mikey to Aunt Lauren and back again.

"Sorry, did we keep you up?" she says. "Mikey and I were taking a bath together. I've always been partial to a Jacuzzi. They remind me of the time Mick, Brian, Marianne, and I holed up at the Chateau Marmont for a wild weekend after one of the Stones' tours."

You hold up your hand and waggle your ring finger. "Can either of you explain this?"

"You insisted on looking after it," Aunt Lauren says. "Mikey had it and was threatening to put it in the pot when we were playing strip poker. You kept giggling and saying 'I don't' to all of us."

"I played strip poker?"

"That's not all you got up to, dear," Aunt Lauren says. She turns to Mikey. "Ready for round three? The water is nice and hot." She winks at you and sashays back into the bathroom.

Mikey looks sheepish. "I think I've met my match." He makes as if to follow her, then turns back. "And do me a favor. My head is killing me. Try to keep the noise down."

"Me?" you say.

He nods. "Last night you two were making a hell of a racket."

"Two? What do you mean by 'you two'?"

The pile of bedding next to you shifts.

Heart in your throat, you pull the covers back and

look down at the man sleeping next to you. A man with tousled black hair. He stretches and yawns.

It's Bruno.

It's all coming back to you. After the game of poker, Lisa and Cat had slipped away together, leaving you and Bruno alone. He'd explained that he and Cat were just friends, and suggested that it would be a shame to waste the champagne in the bridal suite. And then . . .

He grins wickedly and slides an arm around your waist. "Ready for round five?" he asks.

The End

❧ It's Bruno

BRUNO WALKS OUT OF the bathroom, a towel wrapped around his waist.

What have you done?

"Morning," he says, giving you a mischievous grin.

You gulp. "Um . . . Bruno . . . last night . . . did we . . . ?"

"Did we what?"

It looks like you're going to have to spell it out.

The door bursts open, and Lisa walks in. "Surprise!" She's carrying a tray of orange juice, toast, and eggs. "Thought you two could use some breakfast. You were both pretty wasted last night."

She places the tray on the table on the balcony outside. "Lisa," you say. "I think I might have done something really—"

Your heart plummets as Cat enters the room holding a coffeepot. What the hell is going on? "Cat . . . I can explain," you falter, gesturing to Bruno in his towel. Explain what, exactly? That you might have accidentally married her boyfriend?

"There you are, gorgeous," Lisa says. She relieves Cat of the coffeepot, wraps her arms around her neck, and kisses her languorously. "How about coming for a swim?"

You glance at Bruno. He doesn't seem the slightest bit shocked to see his girlfriend kissing Lisa.

"But . . . aren't you and Cat together?" you say to him.

Lisa snorts. "God, you really were out of it last night, weren't you? Cat and Bruno are just good friends."

"Oh," you say, wondering what else you might have missed—and what else went on last night.

Cat and Lisa leave together, laughing.

You wrap a sheet around your naked body. Bruno is sitting at the table on the balcony, and you join him, wincing as the sunlight blasts into your eyes.

"So how did we both end up in here?" you ask.

Bruno hands you a glass of orange juice and butters you a slice of toast as if you're an old married couple. "What's the last thing you remember?"

"Um . . . a bunch of us dancing." You take a sip of juice. It's nectar as it slides down your parched throat. "Bruno . . . Last night, did we . . . ?"

Bruno shakes his head and smiles. "No. You were a bit the worse for wear. We all were. After telling the whole room you loved them, you took me for a walk, saying you wanted to get revenge."

This doesn't sound promising. "Go on."

"You dragged me into a field and pushed me into a cow pie. I needed to shower afterward, and as neither of us could find our room keys, we ended up here. The door was open."

Then you remember the ring. You hold up your hand. "But hang on . . . What about this?"

"Oh, that. Just after the cow-pie incident, you decided all was forgiven between me and you. You convinced Mikey to give you Jane's ring, and insisted that Father Declan marry us."

"I did?"

"You did."

"Why didn't you stop me?"

"Don't worry. It isn't legal. We were just humoring you."

You drop your head into your hands and peer out through your fingers. "And did we consummate our illegal wedding?"

Bruno bites into a piece of toast with relish. "Not yet—but we don't have to check out till noon."

The End

a girl walks into a wedding

☙ You've decided to console Cee Cee

You find Cee Cee curled under a tree on a patch of soft grass beside the lake. Her face is hidden in her arms, her shoulders shuddering with silent sobs.

You're not sure what to do. You've never seen Cee Cee in this state before. Like many control freaks, she's one of life's copers—more likely to be mopping up tears than shedding them.

"Oh, Cee Cee," you say. "Don't take it so hard."

Head still buried in her arms, Cee Cee talks in hiccups. "I just wanted my baby sister to have the most perfect wedding in the world."

"I know, and you've done an incredible job, you really have. But I think Jane's only now figuring out what she really wants."

"I know, and I'm so happy for her. I think that's partly why I'm crying. That and no sleep in weeks. Those fucking doves! I've been more stressed about this wedding than Jane has." She raises her head. Her eyes are damp, but you register that her makeup hasn't run—typical Cee Cee, of course she'd wear waterproof mascara.

"Oh, Cee Cee, don't cry." You lean down and wipe a tear from her cheek. "You'll mess up your makeup, and you've got such a pretty face."

"You think so?"

You look at her properly. You've practically grown up with this woman, so her features are familiar, but you realize you've never really looked at her before. You've never noticed the curve of her cheekbones or the small smile lines around her eyes.

"I do, actually," you say. "I think you have amazing eyes."

"You must also think I'm a giant bitch! I've been a monster this weekend, the way I've been ordering everyone around."

"Okay, so maybe you have been a bit of a wedding-planner-zilla, but who can blame you? You'd have to be a bit bossy and demanding to organize something like this."

You sit down next to Cee Cee and put your arms around her, stroking her hair. She lays her mouth gently against your cheek, and you feel her tears wet on your face. It's a mostly platonic embrace, but you can't help feeling a shiver of something more serious underlying it, too.

Cee Cee pulls away from you, your eyes lock, and something passes between you, some kind of understanding, or maybe it's a wanting. It's all this wedding

a girl walks into a wedding

madness, making you both act out of character. You know she's straight, and so are you, but there's something so comforting in her touch, and so irresistible in her vulnerability, you just want to take away all her hurt.

So you kiss her back, this time on the side of her mouth, and you don't know if it's by accident or on purpose, but as you kiss her, she shifts her face, and you end up kissing each other full on the lips.

After a few moments, you both tentatively explore with your tongues at the same time, and it's a sweet shock to have her tongue in your mouth. It's an entirely new sensation for you—her lips have a softness and suppleness that you're not used to.

You wrap your tongue around hers, both of you uncertain at first—you can tell that it must be as much a new experience for her as it is for you. But it feels so good, you get lost in it, and so does she.

Eventually you lie back on the grass, and Cee Cee follows you down, and you continue to kiss, exploring the contours of each other's faces, lips, and mouths. Cee Cee's hands come up to wander along the front of your dress, and you want her to touch you, but the fabric is like a wall of starch between you.

"This dress is suffocating me!" you gasp, sitting up. "I'm sorry, Cee Cee, I know you aren't having the best wedding ever, but these dresses are a disaster! Yours looks good on you, but mine is an eyesore!"

You see surprise on her face, and there's a second where you're afraid she might start crying again, but then she cracks up laughing. "This whole wedding hasn't been my finest," she admits.

You both giggle, rolling around on the soft grass until you find yourselves kissing again, and you reach behind you and pull the zipper of your dress down, freeing yourself from your chintz straitjacket. She pulls her zipper down, too, and then you both scramble to get each other out of reams of fabric. At last you're both stripped down to your panties.

"What if someone sees us?" Cee Cee asks, pulling away from you.

"I'd rather they saw me like this than in that dress!" you say, reaching for her again.

"I've never done anything like this before," Cee Cee says, her eyes wide.

"Me neither," you gasp as Cee Cee reaches tentatively for your breast, testing the weight of it, and your nipple hardens under her touch. Then she slides her hand down your body, and you feel her fingers trailing over your panties, then dipping inside, stroking your mound at the same time that she explores your mouth with her tongue, while you kiss her back tenderly.

Timidly you slip your own hand down her body, which is so soft and smooth, you want to bury yourself in it. When you reach between her legs, you're surprised to find lace under your fingertips—you would have taken Cee Cee for a plain-cotton girl—but clearly you've misjudged her on a number of counts.

You feel her heat and wetness on your fingertips through the lace, and you go in search of her clit. You

a girl walks into a wedding

can tell you've found it first by her moan, and then by the feel of it pulsing against your fingers.

Mimicking your movements, Cee Cee finds and then rubs your clit, and you feel yourself shudder with bliss. Then it's her turn to go exploring. Slowly, tentatively, she slips a finger inside your pussy. You urge her on with a yes into her mouth, then you copy her, slipping your finger into the soft, warm core of her. She utters a small cry of pleasure as you sink inside her to your knuckle.

Panting, Cee Cee fastens her mouth onto your neck and you run your nails lightly down the smooth skin of her back, drinking in the newness and excitement of everything you're experiencing. You've never felt such soft, wet kisses on your body before. Her body is so similar to yours that you know exactly how to move your fingers to make her writhe.

Then she slips a second finger inside you, and a third, and you take the hint and do the same to her. And you hope she's feeling a tenth of the pleasure you feel as you buck up against her hand. And she must be, because as you caress her sweet spot, she shudders out, "Oh god, oh god!" As she comes, your legs begin to shake, and your pussy contracts around her fingers with an orgasm that would hit eight point nine on the Richter scale.

You both lie back on the grass and stare at the canopy of dappled leaves above. After a comfortable silence, you turn to face each other, and you tuck a strand of hair behind her ear.

"Feeling better?" you ask.

"A lot, actually," Cee Cee says. "What are you thinking?"

"What happens in the country stays in the country?" you say.

"My thoughts exactly. I guess we'd better get back to what's left of the wedding."

"Yeah, I'd kill for a piece of cake," you say, reaching for your dress and getting up so you can step into it.

"You're in luck," says Cee Cee, picking a leaf out of your hair. "I happen to know the wedding planner."

You head back up to the manor together. You feel incredibly relaxed, and even your dress doesn't feel so uncomfortable anymore. As you reach the door to the reception room, which seems to be buzzing with people and music, you notice that Cee Cee is tugging at the bodice of her dress, her breasts bulging over the edges, the capped sleeves cutting off the circulation in her arms. You'd recognize her misery anywhere: She's wearing your dress.

The End

♔ You go to the wedding on your own

"First round is on me," Lisa says.

"I'll have a martini, but hold the olives and make it a double," you say, thinking of that monstrous bridesmaid dress. You need all the stiff drinks you can get to face the prospect of wearing it in public.

"I'm so glad you didn't bring a date—and that we came a night early," Lisa says. She'd convinced you to take an extra day off work for a pre-wedding-stress girls' night out. You'd barely deposited your luggage at the country-manor wedding venue before she dragged you out to the taxi she'd booked to ferry you both to a nearby hotel bar.

"Yeah, it's probably too soon to subject Steve to Jane's family and that bridesmaid dress all in one weekend— he'd run a mile."

"I think you should just have a good time this weekend, go a bit wild. Then when you get back, if this Steve

162

guy turns out to be 'the one,' you can settle down knowing that you've sown your wild oats. I mean, look at this place, it's crawling with cock. It's singles heaven."

You glance around the bar. It's filling up fast. "Is this why you wanted to come here instead of hitting the bar where we're staying?"

"Yep. No one here knows us. We can do what we like."

"What makes you think all these people are single?"

"Please, it's a long weekend, and there are a million weddings happening within a thirty-mile radius. This place is full of people looking to have a good time and not remember it too clearly in the morning. There's something about weddings that make people do things they wouldn't normally do. I think it's all that commitment dangling over their heads. It's the same as people who're inspired to change their lives after they've had a life-threatening accident—it makes them panic and want to have amoral sex."

"I'm so glad you associate long-term commitment with life-threatening accidents."

"I can't help it, I'm on the rebound," Lisa says.

"You're always on the rebound. Speaking of which, don't look now, but do you know that woman?"

Lisa immediately cranes her neck.

"I said don't look now!" you hiss.

"The redhead or the brunette?" Lisa asks.

"The redhead. She keeps looking over here."

Lisa waves at her.

"You know her?" you ask.

"Never set eyes on her in my life. But I have until tomorrow morning to make up for that tragedy."

"I don't know how you do it. I've never had a one-night stand."

"What?" Lisa looks genuinely shocked. "Never?"

You shake your head.

"You don't know what you're missing. There's something incredibly liberating about it. You don't have to worry about tomorrow or the next day, or whether they like you, or whether they'll call back. And the sex is usually awesome."

"It's not that I've never wanted to have one, I've just never had the opportunity."

"Well, if you can't get laid on a weekend like this, then you should go home, buy stretch pants, and get five cats. Who here looks good to you?"

You scan the room. There's a raucous group of men in a corner, but they're not for you—one is in a French maid costume with a tacky ball and chain attached to his ankle.

"What about him?" Lisa asks, nodding toward a man sitting alone at a table. He's older, with the casual confidence of someone who's at home in his own skin. He's wearing dark jeans and a linen shirt. His head is clean-shaven, but in that sexy, intentional way, not in a sad, balding Uncle Vinnie way. And he has light, gray-flecked stubble covering his chin. You're not sure if it's the bald head or the rugged features, but there's something Bruce Willis about him.

"He's okay," you shrug.

"I don't play for that team, but if I did, I'd do him," Lisa says.

"Okay, so he's hot and he's alone, but how do you know he's not a serial killer or even worse, a lawyer?"

"You don't have to settle down with the man and have his babies! Hell, you don't even have to have sex with him, but what's the harm in saying hi? Watch and learn," Lisa says, getting up.

"Wait, I thought this was a girls' night out," you say, grabbing her arm.

"Last time I looked, she was very much a girl," Lisa says, nodding toward the redhead.

"No, Lisa, come back, I hate you!" you call after her, but she's already halfway across the bar. Your face burns as she strikes up a conversation with the older guy. He glances at you, then back at Lisa, then he laughs out loud. He's even more handsome when he laughs. He has one of those sexy dimples in the middle of his chin, and deep lines running from his nose to his mouth. It's too mortifying to watch anymore, so you focus on your martini.

When you finally build up the courage to glance his way again, he's no longer at his table, and Lisa is chatting with the redhead. You're flooded with a mixture of relief and disappointment. Maybe he's married, or maybe he just didn't like the look of you.

You flash back to your hideous bridesmaid dress. What was Jane thinking? Wedding hysteria is the only explanation. Just your luck that when she starts to melt down, the first thing to go is her sense of style. But

a girl walks into a wedding

165

tually dying in the next twenty-four hours of anything other than embarrassment?"

"Actually, my divorce came through today," he says.

"Um . . . congratulations, or commiserations, whichever is required."

He clinks glasses with you and smiles. "Marriage isn't for the fainthearted. I'm a pilot, I wasn't around very much, so she left me. By the time I saw the writing on the wall, it was too late to do anything about it. He's a lot younger than me. I'm coming to terms with it, that's where the whiskey comes in."

"Well, you're a good-looking man and a pilot. You'll be dating again before you know it."

"I haven't been on a date in twenty years. I may be a bit rusty. What have I missed?"

"Not much actually. It's still as archaic as it was back then. The good guys are few and far between, and the ones you want to call back rarely do."

"Oh, come on, a girl as pretty as you must have them dangling from her fingertips."

For some reason, instead of being put off by this cheesy line, your tummy twists in that deliciously knotty way. Or it could be the effects of the second martini. "But seriously," he continues, "you may need to give me a couple of dating pointers. For example, how do I know if a girl likes me?"

You study him carefully. "Well, you have to keep your eye open for some of the more subtle hints. For starters, she might play with her hair," you say, twiddling a strand of hair between your fingers.

"And what if I like her back, how do I let her know?"

"Try touching her arm casually in the course of the conversation. And you have quite a sexy smile, so you should definitely use that."

Without missing a beat, he puts his hand on your arm. "I'll be sure to give that a try."

"Practice makes perfect."

"What about taking things to the next level with someone I think is really sexy? How would I do that?"

"You could ask her out to dinner, seduce her with your charm, and then later, if you're lucky, you might be able to lure her up to your room—if you happened to be staying in this hotel, for example." You can't believe these words are coming out of your mouth. What's gotten into you?

He swirls the ice in his drink, then slays you with another Bruce Willis smile before saying, "I'm starving—how about we get a bite to eat?"

Your heart skips a beat. Of course he's too old for you in the long term, but he's super hot, charming, and a pilot, so would you consider it in the short term? Lisa was right: This is your chance to have a wild one-night stand.

And why not? You've only been on one date with Steve; it's not like you're committed to him. And after that disastrous dress fitting, you could not only do with a confidence boost and a mood lifter, but a little cardio workout, too.

So that's it, then: You're going to sleep with this guy, whether he likes it or not.

You look around for Lisa, who seems to have disappeared. You notice that there's no sign of the redhead, either. You send her a text:

> Don't wait up.

She texts back:

> U neither. And BTW make sure u Do Him Hard
> with a Vengeance.

५ To go to dinner with the pilot, go to page 170.

५ To go straight to his hotel room for your
first-ever one-night stand, go to page 179.

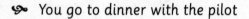

    You go to dinner with the pilot

    "So HOW DO YOU feel about French food?" the pilot asks you.

"I'm a fan," you say. "Except for snails. But I didn't know there was a French restaurant in this town."

"There isn't. But there are plenty to choose from in Paris."

You cock your head at him.

"I don't know about you, but I only really need to be back here by Saturday evening for a family dinner. So I could have you back by then, if that works for you?"

"Wait. You're suggesting we go to France?"

"Oui!"

"Just for dinner?"

"Well, since today is a pretty momentous occasion and I'm a pilot with access to a private jet all weekend and this is my first date in twenty years, I thought maybe we should make it a little more memorable than the local burger joint. What do you say?"

"But surely you're not allowed to fly after drinking?" you ask, nodding at the whiskey he's nursing.

"I couldn't possibly fly; I have a guest to entertain. And it just so happens my copilot is on standby the whole weekend. Wait, what about your passport?"

"It's at my hotel. I never leave home without it—I may or may not have been a secret agent in a previous life."

"Well, then it's entirely up to you. Donkey burger at the place down the road or Alain Ducasse for anything except snails?"

A million thoughts whip through your head. You could be back in time for the wedding, and you really do only live once . . .

"Let's do it!" you say.

"Fantastic. The name's Jack, by the way." He touches your cheek, then calls to the bartender for the bill.

Paris. In a jet. With a pilot. "Yippee-ki-yay, mother-fucker," you whisper under your breath.

"THAT'S QUITE SOME BATHTUB," you say, standing in the door of the suite's immaculate bathroom, looking at an enormous and elegant tub that's just begging for champagne, bubbles, and an hour-long soak.

"Do you think there's room for two?" Jack says from behind you, lodging his chin on your shoulder.

"I think we'd be wrong not to try and see."

a girl walks into a wedding

"I'll get the champagne," Jack says as you turn on the taps, running your fingers through the water to get the temperature right, your heart starting to race with anticipation. You light the candles strategically placed around the bathroom, then decant the contents of a bottle of bubbles into the water. Steam and scent fills the room.

You and Jack arrived in Paris just in time to enjoy a spectacular and snail-free late dinner at Le Cinq, the hotel's Michelin-star restaurant, and despite the five courses and vintage wine, you're not even slightly drowsy. You gaze out of the sash window, which frames a view of the skyline and the Champs-Élysées, elegant fairy lights glittering in the trees lining the boulevard.

You can barely believe you're here. You can't wait to tell Lisa about your adventure, starting with the flight in the Learjet—who knew such a relatively small plane could be so luxurious? Perhaps tomorrow you'll have time to explore the arrondissement's upscale boutiques and buy her a present to thank her for introducing you to Jack. It's turning into the best one-night stand ever—beyond even Lisa's wildest dreams.

Jack returns and hands you a glass of champagne. "To Paris," he says.

You clink your glass against his, and both take a sip. Then he places his glass down on the edge of the bath, and steps toward you, taking your head in his hands as he kisses you with the kind of passion usually reserved for classic books and black-and-white movies.

You push his jacket off his shoulders and undo the

buttons of his shirt. He tugs your dress up over your head, and you both slip wordlessly out of your shoes.

You feel momentarily shy standing almost naked in front of him, so you cover your chest with your arms. Sensing your shyness, Jack turns and dims the light so the room is bathed in the flickering caress of candle-light. As he does so, you slip out of your panties and step carefully into the bath, sinking into the oil-slickened water, feeling it envelop your naked body, bubbles covering you.

You shift forward in the bath and turn off the taps as Jack climbs in behind you. With a contented sigh, you lean back against him, his legs on either side of your body, relishing the strength of his chest against your back.

He takes a large, soft sponge and lathers it up. Then, starting at your shoulder, he runs it slowly down your one arm, and then the other. Returning to your neck, he sponges his way up to your ear, and then back down again, stopping to soap the sponge once again before running it down your chest, then first over one breast, and then the other. The scrape of the sponge pauses for the briefest moment before it passes your nipple, which hardens to a nub the second he wipes the silken lather over it.

Jack's hand sinks into the heated water, and the sponge travels down your belly while he caresses your earlobe with his other hand. Then slowly, slowly he runs the sponge over your pussy, and you drop your head back onto his shoulder and close your eyes, pleasure mounting as his cock hardens. You can feel it pressing into the base of your spine where your bodies meet, just a skin of warm water between you.

You let out a little groan as Jack rubs the sponge between your legs once, then again slightly harder before returning it to your collarbone and starting his journey once more. First each arm, and then your breasts again, this time running his hand over one breast, his fingertips teasing the nipple while he strokes the sponge over the other.

He kisses your neck as he drops the sponge back down into the water, his other hand still entertaining your nipple, and you feel the sponge back between your legs. He runs it up and down your slit over and over again, increasing the pressure on every pass. You tilt your pelvis up toward the sponge, trying to increase the pressure against your clit, and you take small bites at the side of Jack's neck and across his earlobe, urging him on with small moans, your breath quickening.

You squeal as you feel a rush of water against your skin, as a dozen or so strategically placed spa jets come to life. One is angled so that the strong stream of water strikes your pussy. You place your feet on either side of the taps, so the jet hits your clit directly. Jack abandons the sponge, and you feel his fingers slipping inside you as the jet of water pulses against you. First just the one finger, and then, when you can barely stand it anymore, you feel him filling you up.

Your skin is soft and oily against his as you buck your hips into his hand and the strong jet of water, until your pussy clenches with an orgasm that has your fingers grasping at the sides of the tub, every muscle taut for a split second before you peak. And then you relax back into his body with a gasp, your eyes closed, the bubbled water sloshing over your chest and spilling out onto the black-and-white-checkered floor.

The jets subside as you gather your senses, and you hear the water start to drain as Jack pulls the plug with his toe. You lean forward as he stands, the water sheeting off his muscular thighs. You can't take your eyes off his body as he steps out of the bath and wraps a white towel around his waist.

Then he reaches for another towel. You stand, your legs still shaking, and he takes your hand to steady you as you climb out of the tub. Standing in the middle of the bath mat in the flickering candlelight, Jack runs the towel down your body, drying you bit by bit. First he pats the towel around your shoulders, drying each arm, and then he runs the towel across your breasts, drying each one slowly and with great care.

Then he drops to his knees in front of you and slowly towels your belly and then each of your legs, finally returning to your pussy and patting it gently dry, his erection making a large tent underneath his towel.

Then he stands again and reaches for a George V–monogrammed robe, which he wraps around you, kissing you passionately again, and you feel like putty in his hands as he leads you into the bedroom.

The baroque-style bed is the size of a small island. You place a hand against Jack's chest and push so that he falls back onto the bed, sinking deep into the luscious white duvet—you're sure the thread count of the linen must be in the millions.

You retrieve the champagne and pour two fresh glasses, slipping a condom out of your bag at the same time. You return to the bed and hand Jack his glass. He sips as he watches you, a small smile crossing his face as you walk toward him with a tray bearing strawberries and a silver bowl filled with cream.

"Now it's your turn," you say, standing at the foot of the bed, slowly letting your robe slide to the floor, and he lies back, his strong arms raised behind his head.

You clamber onto the bed alongside him, take a strawberry by the small green stem, then dip it into the cream, scooping up a dollop on the end. Using the strawberry like a paintbrush, you run it along the soft, sensitive skin on the underside of his arm, just above his armpit, painting the number one in cream on his skin. Then you scoop up more cream with the tip of the strawberry and paint the number two on his stomach. He watches with desire in his eyes as you repeat the process to paint the number three on one nipple and four on the other. And then you pull the towel from around his hips, and slowly paint the number five just below his belly button, beneath his cock, which is straining for the ceiling. You raise an eyebrow, noticing that it has a definite bend to the left.

Then you kneel above him and get to work, slowly lapping up the cream, starting at number one, which

Helena L. Paige

has you licking at the smooth silken skin above his armpit, while you trail your fingers down the sensitive skin on his side, feeling goose bumps pop to the surface as he shivers with delight. Then you straddle him carefully and drop your head down to his stomach to lap up number two before making your way over to his nipple for number three. By the time you reach number four, still taking your time, you can practically hear his heart racing.

Jack's breath is coming in quick pants, and you can tell the torture is almost too much for him, so it's a good thing number five is next. You drop your head down to just below his belly button, lapping up the number five, starting at the top of the number and taking it in one long lick, then continuing from the bottom of the five down onto the tip of his cock, which is as solid as a rock. Then you look up at him as you run your tongue from the tip all the way along the hard curve of it, down to the base of his cock and then back up again, before sinking your mouth over him and taking the whole generous heft of him in your mouth. Then with your palm wrapped around the base of his cock, you pump it as you suck it.

When you're sure he can't take another second of your mouth, you crawl up his body again, reach for the condom you dropped on the tray, tear it open, and wrap it quickly onto his cock, while he whispers your name in your ear and begs to come inside you.

You hover over him and then drop down slowly onto

him, his cock filling you inch by inch. He starts to thrust up into you as you rotate your hips, feeling the head of his cock rub against your G-spot.

His pounding becomes harder and faster and more furious, hitting your sweet spot every single time, and you arch your back as you start to feel yourself going over the edge. Your orgasm beats around and through you in waves, and he follows closely after you with a series of ramming thrusts that reverberate in your pussy as you come. Satiated, you drop down onto his chest and feel his skin soft against yours, the brush of his stubble on your forehead.

Viva la France, you think. So far Jane's wedding is the best wedding you've ever been to, and it hasn't even started yet.

The End

Helena L. Paige

You go straight to the pilot's hotel room

HE SWIPES THE KEY card and lets you in ahead of him, using the dimmer to keep the lights low. You feel giddy as you step into his suite, hardly able to believe you're doing this.

"Drink?" he asks, walking toward the minibar.

"Please," you say, doing a quick survey of the lavish suite, all modern understated luxury. His broad shoulders ripple under his shirt as he pulls out a couple of small bottles, and you can't wait to feel the shape of his muscles under his skin, and his lips on yours. You've always loved that moment before a first kiss. All that flirting and flutter of nerves, the buildup of expectation, the slow burn escalating in your panties.

You try to decide where to sit. The bed feels too obvious and the armchair too lonely, so you settle onto the sofa. He hands you a glass and then hovers. You can tell he's nervous, and it's kind of cute.

"So, when you start dating . . ." you say.

"Yes?"

"If you manage to get a woman up to your room, it's okay to sit next to her on the sofa. If you want."

He smiles and joins you, then without saying anything else, he places a big, warm hand on the back of your neck and leans toward you. You kiss, and it's urgent but gentle at the same time. There's no awkward bumping of chins or knocking of teeth; your faces fit together perfectly. His tongue does a round of your mouth, and you return the favor. The kiss ends, and he pulls away from you a little.

"You'll have to be gentle with me, okay? I wasn't kidding—I haven't done this in a long time." His vulnerability is touching and a turn-on.

"Don't worry, this won't hurt a bit." This time you kiss him hungrily, feeling his stubble burn against your cheeks. You place both hands on his chest and feel the tautness of his muscles underneath. Your fingers slip between the buttons of his shirt, eager to feel his skin.

He fumbles at the straps of your dress, running his hand across your chest and around your neckline, his fingers slipping under your bra strap, but not quite straying onto your breasts.

Then you go back to kissing like a pair of teenagers for what feels like hours, getting to know the shape of each other's bodies. At some stage he sweeps you onto his lap, and you feel his erection against you through his jeans.

As you kiss, you slowly undo the rest of his buttons,

and he peels the straps of your dress and your bra lower and lower until you can feel his skin against yours.

"How am I doing?" he mumbles into your neck at some point.

"Not bad for a beginner," you murmur back.

"I'll show you beginner," he says, slipping his arms around you and laying you down on your back on the couch, kneeling over you, his body pressed against yours as you kiss some more. You're going to have a hard time explaining your beard rash to the girls tomorrow. An allergic reaction to shellfish maybe. But you can't think about that as he runs his mouth down over your breasts, taking one nipple gently between his teeth, and his fingers slide up under your skirt and rub over the fabric of your panties. You moan as you anticipate what's coming next.

❧ If you want to go down on him, go to page 182.

❧ If you want him to go down on you, go to page 185.

a girl walks into a wedding

❧ You want to go down on him

"WAIT," YOU WHISPER, AND he raises his head and looks at you.

You wriggle out from under him. Then you smile like a lynx, toss one of the sofa cushions onto the floor, and kneel between his legs. He bends over you and kisses you so deeply that your head reels. When at last you break apart, you undo the buttons of his jeans and slide them down his legs, then toss them over your shoulder.

You kiss him again and rake your fingernails down and then back up both his thighs, feeling the muscles go taut. Then, still kissing him, you reach for his cock, releasing it from his boxers and grasping it in the palm of your hand. You've never been this brazen before, but you're loving the reaction you're getting. He sucks in a breath and then groans happily. The skin of his cock is so soft to the touch, it's almost silken. It's the ideal size, but to your surprise, it has a definite bend to the left. More curve than the Leaning Tower of Pisa, but less than a boomerang. Fascinated by your discovery, you lower your head and take just the tip of it into your mouth. He groans again and clutches the sofa cushions so tightly his knuckles go white. This is going to be fun, you think.

Slowly you take his cock into your mouth, bit by bit, then return your hand to the base of it, bobbing your head as you run your hand up and down in time with your sucking. Then, when he least expects it, you alter the speed of your attack and devour him whole again. His groans escalate and his hands lace into your hair, massaging the back of your neck with strong fingers.

Then you lick the length of him in one tantalizingly slow move, before taking him in your mouth again and starting over from the beginning, using his moans to gauge his excitement, and gradually increasing the intensity and speed of your movements until he's bucking to meet your mouth and begging for you not to stop, not to ever stop. But you do, because you can.

Then you climb back onto the sofa and straddle him, nuzzling the nape of his neck. Still wearing your panties, now soaked through, you ride him, the underside of his hard, pulsating cock rubbing against your slit. The feeling is exquisite, and he holds you and nips at your neck as you ride him faster and faster, until you're bucking against each other for long delectable minutes. It crosses your mind briefly to find a condom so he can slip inside you, but the thought of stopping what you're doing is impossible, the sensation is so phenomenal. So you build up speed instead, and the friction between you is insanely pleasurable—maybe it's the pronounced bend of his cock that makes it fit so perfectly against the curve of your pussy, so he's able to rub your clit over and over, and you can't stop yourself from coming, and then almost immediately he comes in a great release of energy, cries of pleasure racking both your bodies.

You shudder as you sink beside each other on the couch, and he snakes his arms around you as your pulses slowly jog back to normal.

❧ Go to page 188.

Helena S. Paige

❧ You want him to go down on you

HE KNEELS OVER YOU lying on the couch and uses four fingers of one hand to rub up and down your slit over your panties. You close your eyes and thrust your hips to meet the strokes of his hand. At the same time, his lips travel the length of your neck, visiting your breasts and nipples slowly, teasingly, and then moving back to your mouth. Soon his hands slip inside your undies, and he murmurs when he finds how wet you are. You feel him shift his body as he drops to his knees on the floor beside the sofa.

He slips your panties off, then sinks his head between your legs, nuzzling at your mound, nipping very gently.

You can feel his stubble rubbing against your thighs, the prickle of it heightening your sensitivity. At last you feel his open mouth on your pussy, and he licks you just once before taking your lips gently between his teeth, tugging on them, and then he's licking you properly, over and over again like an ice cream cone, dipping his tongue inside you, his hands massaging both your inner thighs. You raise your hips to draw his tongue deeper.

"Oh my god," you moan, squirming as he slips a finger inside you at the same time as his tongue keeps flicking and teasing at you. "Don't stop," you urge as he briefly takes your clit between his teeth, which is the very best kind of agony.

You run a hand over the top of his head, and with your other you grip a sofa cushion as he keeps on licking, and the sensations are so intense that you can't tell what's tongue and what's fingers anymore, you only know that if he stops doing exactly what he's doing right now, you might just die. Before you can even try to control it, your orgasm blows through your body, making every muscle quiver uncontrollably.

As your body is racked by miniature quakes, you shift to make room for him on the sofa, and he lies alongside the length of you, wrapping his arms around you tightly as you shudder out the last of your orgasm. He pushes your hair out of your face and smiles at you, and you reach down, feeling for the button of his jeans.

Then you find his cock, which is as hard as a boulder, and run your hand from the base to the tip, surprised to discover that it has a considerable bend to the left. The skin is as soft as silk, and you love the feel of it, so powerful in your palm. You run your hand up and down it, slowly at first, then, as he starts to groan, you speed up your pace until he can't help bucking into your hand, moaning as he devours your mouth and neck with

Helena L. Paige

kisses, your hand moving faster and faster until he comes with an orgasm so intense it rocks his entire body, and he shouts out in pleasure.

Then you turn and nestle your back against him so you can spoon, your eyes closed, feeling his pulse beating against your back as he holds you tightly, catching his breath until it matches the slow rise and fall of yours. So this is what a one-night stand feels like, you think. Wow. You could get used to this.

❧ Go to page 188.

YOU MUST HAVE FALLEN asleep. As you open your eyes, you remember you're in a fabulous hotel suite with the Bruce Willis look-alike pilot you met in the bar. The one with the bendy penis. You can feel him breathing evenly behind you, deep in sleep.

You slip off the edge of the sofa and crawl guerrilla-style along the floor, grabbing at stray items of clothing as you go. You wonder about leaving your phone number, but that would defeat the object of a one-night stand. Lisa was right, it was fun for a night, something to cheer you up. And at least by leaving, you're cutting out any awkward post-action conversation. This man has barely been divorced for five minutes. Someone on the rebound is definitely not the kind of guy you're after.

A bellhop stops and stares blatantly as he catches you slipping on your shoes outside the hotel room.

"Morning, nothing to see here," you say as you head for the reception desk, where you have to ask the concierge to call you a taxi.

The taxi driver smiles knowingly as you climb in and ask him to take you back to your hotel in what is clearly a cocktail dress and heels—not exactly suitable attire for eight in the morning.

You assess your face in your makeup mirror, finding that your mascara is clumped, your eyeliner has smudged, and fixing your hair would be impossible without industrial-strength equipment. You do your best with your fingers (why is there never a tissue or a comb in your bag when you need one?), but the majority of the damage will have to be dealt with using heavy-duty makeup remover back at your hotel. Thank goodness you slipped out before Bruce Willis's stunt double woke up. You might have given him a heart attack looking like this.

It was dark when you arrived last night, and you hadn't realized the full magnificence of the venue where the wedding is being held. As the taxi putters down a long graveled drive, you see a stone manor house, complete with chapel, formal rose gardens, lawns that sweep up to a folly and then down to a glimmering lake complete with serene swans—there are even sheep grazing in a meadow beyond the water. You expect the theme music for *Downton Abbey* to start playing any minute.

The taxi driver drops you off just as a black van draws up, drum 'n' bass leaking through the windows. A guy dressed in skinny black jeans, a tight T-shirt, and boots jumps out of the driver's seat and shoots you an appreciative glance.

"Morning," he says. "You here for the wedding?"

"Um . . . yes. You?"

"I'm the DJ."

"DJ Salinger?" Jane's assessment of his hotness was right on the money.

"The one and only. Forgot your luggage?" He grins at you, and you smile back. It's clear he knows exactly what you've been up to and isn't judging.

"To be honest, I'm trying to slip in without anyone noticing."

"Been there, done that," he says. "If you wait while I unpack my gear, I'll help smuggle you in."

You're about to take him up on his offer when you see a motorcycle powering down the drive, followed by several cars. No doubt other guests arriving for the wedding weekend. "Don't worry," you say, with a twinge of regret. "I'll be fine."

"Cool. See you later . . . I hope."

You mutter a greeting to the receptionist and speed-walk toward the hallway that leads to the rooms. But you only manage a few steps before you hear a voice calling your name. You hesitate. It's Jane's mom. Busted!

❧ If you make a run for it, go to page 191.

❧ If you face the music, go to page 193.

190

❧ You make a run for it

THE THOUGHT OF BEING discovered by your best friend's mom, sneaking back to your hotel after a night spent doing the dirty with a stranger, is mortifying. You speed up to a brisk hobble in your killer heels. If she gives you a hard time later, you can always say you were listening to your iPod—those headphones get smaller every year.

"Oh, there you are," says Cee Cee, emerging from a doorway, her arms full of dress bags, blocking your escape. "If you're not busy, you can help me steam the creases out of the bridesmaids' dresses. And I've got the flower girls' outfits here as well."

What to do? The last thing you want is to spend the morning ironing that sartorial nightmare you have to wear on Sunday. It looks like you're caught between a frock and a red face. You choose the lesser of the two evils. "I can't," you say. "Your mom needs me." Before Cee Cee can respond, you turn and call, "Coming, Mrs. B.!"

❧ Go to page 193.

Helena S. Paige

✋ You face the music

"MORNING, BUTTERCUP!" JANE'S MOTHER carols, fluttering toward you in a bright orange velour tracksuit. "Isn't it just beautiful here?" she gushes. "I'm so glad you're here safe and sound. Did you arrive last night? How did you sleep? Do you have a lovely room? Ours is just heavenly." She barely leaves you time to nod in response. On the bright side, she doesn't seem to have picked up on the fact that you're wearing a cocktail dress and sequined heels at eight thirty in the morning.

"Come and say hello to everyone," she says, taking you by the wrist and dragging you toward a sunny breakfast conservatory. The DJ, who's lugging boxes of equipment into one of the adjoining function suites, mouths "Good luck" at you.

You'll need it. As you and Mrs. B. enter the room, everyone seated around a large breakfast table stops talking midsentence, and stares at you.

"Morning, darling," Jane's aunt Lauren greets you, giving your cocktail dress a knowing—and slightly approving—glance. She's unshockable, having been almost solely responsible for putting the word "swinging" into the term "swinging sixties."

"Morning," you say. Then you nod at Jane's dad, who is layering his toast with jelly as if he's a builder cementing bricks.

Jane's mother introduces you to Tom's mother and new partner (who is a good twenty years her junior), then gestures at a raffishly handsome man seated next to Jane's dad. "And this is Father Declan. He's doing the honors on Sunday."

So *this* is Father Declan. Holy cow. No wonder Jane had a crush on him as a teenager. This man can't be a priest—he's too hot. He has that dark Celtic coloring, his eyes fringed by the thickest, blackest eyelashes you've ever seen on a man. His hair just touches his collar, and his strong jaw is speckled with something that's halfway between a beard and unruly stubble. He's wearing jeans and an open-necked black shirt.

"Nice to meet you," he says, an unmistakable lilt in his voice.

"You can't be a priest," you blurt out. Dammit. You hadn't planned on actually saying that aloud. "I mean, you're not wearing a collar," you try to recover.

He smiles, and his eyes crinkle, his whole face lighting up. And you suddenly want to find religion, say as many Hail Marys as it takes, as long as you can follow this man wherever he leads you.

"I promise to wear it to the wedding as proof," he says in that beautiful voice, and your legs turn to jelly.

"And of course you remember Bruno, Jane's brother," Mrs. B. says, gesturing at a dark-haired man sitting next to a slender woman at the end of the table. "He's a real TV-series writer now."

You'd forgotten that he was flying in for the wedding. The Bruno you remember was overweight and pimply, smelled a bit ripe, and had a nasty habit of shoving you into cow pies. Still, life seems to have been good to him. He's still a little on the stocky side, but he's definitely shaped up since you last saw him and improved his dress sense, too. What he does still have is a mischievous smile, a shock of jet-black hair, and eyebrows that have a life of their own.

"Hi, Stinky," says Bruno. "This is Cat." He puts an arm around the woman seated next to him. She's at least half a head taller than Bruno and beautiful in a subtle way. She smiles warmly at you, and you find yourself taking an instant liking to her.

"No date?" Bruno smirks.

You open your mouth to retort when Aunt Lauren says, "You're keeping your options open, aren't you, darling?" You blush, remembering last night's shenanigans. That's one way of putting it.

"Well, it's nice to see you up and about so early, dear," Mrs. B. says.

"I was . . . I . . . I went for a walk." You glance down at your shoes. "I left my sneakers at home."

a girl walks into a wedding

"Bullshit," Bruno says, doing that childish thing of covering up a word with a pretend cough.

You feel something sticky on your leg and look down to find a child standing with one hand on your calf and a finger shoved up her nose.

"No!" a woman's voice scolds. "No fingers up your nose! How many times do I have to tell you!" And then, "Tokyo! Stop poking your sister! No, Manhattan! Put down that knife this instant!"

Suddenly the breakfast room is crawling with little people. Jane's cousin Noe air-kisses you as she swoops down on an errant toddler who is about to put a lethal-looking knife into her mouth. Noe is Noeleen, but she's been Noe since high school. Until she and her high school sweetheart, Dom, got engaged, when they became Domino, one indistinguishable person, never to be individuals again.

Just then Dom arrives, staggering under enough luggage for a trek across Outer Mongolia, and what appears to be a large hamster cage. Surely that's not a rat inside? It is, and a large piebald one at that.

"Does Cee Cee know you're bringing an extra guest to the wedding?" you ask, nodding at the rat.

Dom sighs. "Meet Yodabell. And no, don't ask me to explain the name. The girls insisted we bring him."

While the kids mob their father and pet, you steal sideways looks at Father Declan. Somebody needs to write a letter to Rome to rectify this situation. He's far too hot to be off the market.

"Morning!" Mikey—Tom's best man—saunters into

the room carrying a motorcycle helmet and a suit bag over his shoulder. He's tanned and rumpled, as if he's just stepped out of a Jeep in the African bush. Mikey's a hotshot surgeon who does stints with Doctors Without Borders, so you've never spent very much time with him. But Jane's been warning you off him for years—his rampant womanizing is legendary.

Mikey greets the others, then homes in on you. He gives you an unnecessarily tight squeeze and whispers "Rough night?" in your ear, with the knowing tone of a man who recognizes a fellow walk-of-shamer. Fortunately it's a rhetorical question, so you don't have to explain yourself.

Bruno glances at you and murmurs something in his date's ear. You feel a jab of irritation. Who is he to make snarky remarks about you?

"Well, these digs aren't too shabby," Mikey says, surveying the property, which extends beyond the conservatory into old-fashioned country gardens, complete with fountains and lavender hedges. "Who's up for a breakfast cocktail?" He raises a hand to get the waitress's attention. "Nurse, we're going to need some drinks, stat."

"I think I'm just going to head up to my room," you say.

"Don't forget the bachelorette party tonight," Aunt Lauren calls.

"Need any help?" Mikey says. "What's on the menu? Male strippers, cocktails with penis straws, that kind of thing?"

Aunt Lauren blows him a lascivious kiss. "Oh, I think we can manage something better than that."

"Don't be so sure. Cee Cee's in charge," you say.

"Oh dear," she sighs, drifting off for a cigarette and to flirt with the young hotel bellhop.

"Are you sure I can't bend your rubber arm to join me for a cocktail?" Mikey asks. "We could go for Sex on the Beach, or a Slippery Nipple. I think you'd enjoy both."

Yuck, you think. Mikey really is a parody of a womanizer. "Does that cheesy stuff really work?" you ask him.

He smirks, unfazed.

"And anyway, last time I looked there was no beach out here," you say.

"Visit me in room thirty-three, and I'll show you how wrong you are," he whispers.

As if, you think. You're not that kind of woman. But then again . . . until last night you weren't the kind of woman who had one-night stands.

"See you ladies tonight," you announce to the room, making a point of avoiding eye contact with Mikey and Bruno. How is it that Jane's brother has managed to stay as annoying as he was when you were eleven?

❧ Go to page 199.

❧ It's the bachelorette party

"WHAT'S WORSE THAN MADONNA singing 'Like a Virgin'?" Lisa has to shout to be heard over the music.

"What?" you shout back.

"Jane's aunt Lauren singing 'Like a Virgin'! Somebody kill me now!"

You burst out laughing, watching as Aunt Lauren gyrates onstage, her eyes fixed on the young bartender, who's looking flustered but intrigued.

Lisa waves at the bartender, who drags his eyes away from the sight of Aunt Lauren breathing heavily into the microphone. "Tequilas all around, please."

Cee Cee's the only one who isn't getting into the swing of things. She'd wanted to go to a spa, or have a quiet girls' night in, but Lisa and Aunt Lauren overruled her, insisting that everyone head to a local country pub for a night of bad karaoke and lethal cocktails.

The place is packed, and you flick your eyes around nervously, hoping you won't run into the pilot you abandoned. That would be awkward.

"How much fun is this?" Jane yells over the hubbub.

"So much fun," you say, trying to sound convincing, but she knows how you feel about karaoke—you don't even sing in the shower, let alone in front of at least a hundred people.

"I can't believe I'm getting married this weekend!" Jane hiccups.

"I can't believe it either!" you say.

"Look, they've got 'Bohemian Rhapsody'!" Noe screeches as she flips through the file. "I love that song!" As the clearly not-a-virgin finishes her rendition, Noe races onto the stage in fits of champagne giggles to murder another unsuspecting number.

"To my last nights of freedom!" Jane toasts, knocking back a shot of tequila. "You know you're my besht friend in the whole wide world, right?" she slurs.

"Yes, and now my best friend is getting married."

"Yeah . . . about that . . ." She picks at a bar mat. "What if I'm making the biggest mistake of my life?"

A prickle of concern runs down your spine. "All brides think that before they get married," you hedge.

"No, but what if I really am?" Jane says, her bottom lip quivering.

"You're just having cold feet. It's completely normal."

"I know Tom's not the most exciting guy in the world. But he'll make a great father."

"Oh my god, you're not pregnant, are you?"

"What? Of course not! I mean, down the line. I'm just not so sure that he's . . ." she stumbles.

"What?"

"Nothing, it's nothing. He loves me, and he's a good man, and anyway it's too late, we'll never get our deposit back now."

"What do you mean? Are you considering calling it off?" You're horrified, although there's an infinitesimally small part of you that is perking up at the thought of being spared the Diabolical Dress of Sprigged Disaster.

"No, it's just . . . I've been thinking about stuff . . ." Jane says.

"What kind of stuff?"

"You know I've never been with anyone else, right?"

"Yeah, but you've kissed other guys."

"Kissed, yes, but I've never *been*-been with anyone else, not in *that* way."

"Jane, you started going out with Tom your freshman year of college. I'd be worried if you'd slept with fifty other guys!"

"But what if the sex is really, really bad, and I just don't know because I've never slept with anyone else?"

"Is the sex really, really bad?" you ask.

"I don't know. That's my point. What if it's actually awful?"

"For crying out loud, Jane. I think you'd know if it was awful!"

"But don't you see? I've got nothing to compare it to!" Jane drops her head into her arms.

You rub her back and wonder whether you should share your own concerns about Tom. On the one hand she's so drunk, chances are she won't remember it in the morning. But on the other hand, what if she does remember? You don't want to be responsible for ending a marriage before it's even started. And so what if you're not that crazy about Tom? Like the pilot said, you're not the one marrying him.

Jane lifts her head. "Tell me honestly, do you think I'm doing the right thing?"

❧ If you decide to tell Jane what you really think, go to page 203.

❧ If you keep it to yourself, go to page 205.

Helena L. Paige

202

🌑 **You tell Jane what you really think**

 "So," JANE BADGERS. "Do you honestly think I'm doing the right thing?"

"Define 'right,'" you start.

"Okay . . . do you think Tom is the right man for me? Do you like him?" Jane asks.

"Sure, I like him."

"But do you *like*-like him?"

"No, but I'm not the one who's marrying him. I don't have to *like*-like him."

"Okay . . . then do you like him for me?"

It's now or never. Rather have this conversation now, than in ten years' time.

"Jane, I think he's . . ."

"Oh my god, I love this song!" Jane leaps up and runs to the stage where her mom and aunt Lauren are busy slaughtering the chorus of "Wild Thing."

You wonder if she left the table so abruptly because

she didn't want to hear what you had to say. Ah, well. Now's not the time to be heaping further doubts on what are hopefully just normal pre-wedding jitters. She probably won't even remember any of this in the morning. Some things are simply best left unsaid. Saved by the Troggs.

❧ Go to page 209.

Helena L. Paige

🕭 You keep your opinion to yourself

 "Is TOM GOOD TO YOU?" you ask.

"Yes, absolutely," Jane says.

"Does he make you happy?"

"Most of the time."

"Is he honest?" you say.

"To a fault."

"Most important of all: Does he have a big willy?" you ask, straight-faced.

Jane bursts out laughing, then bounces out of her seat, shouting, "Oh my god, I love this song!" She darts off to join Lisa and Cat, who are singing Katy Perry's "I Kissed a Girl."

So you didn't tell her what you really thought. But then will Jane remember any of this in the morning?

- If you want to stick around for one last song, go to page 207.

- If you're all pretty wasted and it's time to head back to the hotel, go to page 209.

Helena L. Paige

❧ You want to stay for one last song

IT HAD TO HAPPEN. Someone has chosen "I Will Survive." Karaoke meets bachelorette party: It's a law of the universe.

You all huddle around the mikes, singing the lyrics everyone knows and mumbling the ones you don't, because it's too late and you've all had too many drinks to be following that tiny little ball on that tiny little screen. Most of the crowd joins in, and some of them have even formed a small mosh pit in front of the stage.

As you hit the high point of the second chorus, the microphones go dead. Aunt Lauren keeps on singing, not realizing or caring that she's doing an unplugged version, but the rest of you stop singing, and the crowd moans in disappointment. Jane and Lisa tap the microphones they're holding, but there's no sound, and the backing track carries on playing alone.

Karaoke Guy fiddles with a few buttons, then shrugs. "Sorry, ladies, must have shorted out or something."

You all traipse off the stage. As you walk past the DJ, you catch him plugging in a little jack on his deck. The green light on your mike fizzes back to life. You glare at him and he stares back, unfazed.

You can't blame him: How many times can a man survive a bad rendition of "I Will Survive"?

And it's late, you're all a little drunk, it's time to head back to the hotel, anyway.

❧ Go to page 209.

Helena S. Paige

ॐ You go back to the hotel

DAMMIT. YOU CAN'T FIND your key. You dig through your bag, but no luck. You make your way to the reception desk, but it appears to be closed for the night.

God knows where Lisa is, and Jane's nowhere to be seen—she and Aunt Lauren took a separate taxi. You briefly consider knocking at the infamous room 33— Mikey's "love nest." Maybe you could fake an injury and have him take a look at it. You could play doctor. No. You're not that drunk. You'll never be that drunk.

Should you call the night manager? It's just too late. Your only option is to try to get into your room via the hotel balconies. You're sure you left the French doors un-locked. You take off your heels and head outside to the front lawn.

Tucking the skirt of your dress into your underwear, you climb up and over the balustrade of the balcony and tiptoe past the first room. Which one is yours? The second or third one down—something like that. Thankfully the French doors to the third room are open, and you slip inside.

You click on the bedside light, but instead of seeing your suitcase on the floor, there's a leather jacket and motorcycle helmet.

You've found yourself in room 33 after all.

You hear a key in the door. Shit, how are you going to explain what you're doing in Mikey's room in the middle of the night? You flee back to the balcony, pausing as you hear shuffling and heavy breathing. Mikey isn't alone. He murmurs, "Oh baby!"

And then you hear a woman's voice murmuring his name back.

You bite your tongue to stop yourself from crying out. You'd recognize that voice anywhere. You reel back onto the balcony, narrowly avoiding a collision with the wrought-iron table.

You play the night back in your mind, trying to understand what you've just witnessed. Yes, Jane was having cold feet, but Mikey is Tom's best man, for fuck's sake.

You dart toward the next room—this one has to be yours—haul open the door and dive onto the bed, burying your face in the pillow. Oh god, what a mess. "Christ!" you say.

"Jesus!" a man's voice exclaims.

Your heart does its best to leap out of your mouth. You blink as a bedside lamp clicks on and your eyes adjust to the light. What the hell? Father Declan is lying under the covers next to you. "Jesus, Mary, and Joseph!" he says.

"I thought you weren't allowed to say that," you blurt out.

"Of course I bloody am, especially under the circumstances. What are you doing in my room?"

"Your room? This is *my* room!"

You look around and it dawns on you that it isn't actually your room after all. There's a black shirt with a dog collar hanging on the wardrobe door, and on the bedside table is a rosary and a missal. And what looks like a hip flask.

Father Declan kicks back the covers and stands up. He's only wearing a pair of boxer shorts, and even though you're in shock, a tiny part of your brain registers that he has a fantastic body, with broad shoulders tapering down into a long, lean torso. He must sense your gaze, because he goes over to his suitcase and pulls on a T-shirt before coming to sit beside you.

"Are you all right? You're terribly pale," he says, more gently.

Tears prickle, and to your mortification, you start to sniffle. "I'm sorry, I've had a bad night."

Father Declan produces an old-fashioned clean white hanky from somewhere and hands it to you. "Here, blow," he says, putting a warm hand on your back. "You gave me the fright of my life. I need a drink. Why don't I get you one, too, and then you can tell me what happened."

You prop yourself up against the pillows as he pours

a splash of whiskey from his flask into one of the hotel's heavy crystal glasses and hands it to you.

"What has you so upset?" he asks, sitting beside you on the bed.

"I've just seen something really shocking," you say. "We were at karaoke, and we all had too much to drink . . ." You pause. "Look, this is super confidential. Jane is my oldest friend. I have to know that you won't tell anyone."

"I promise nothing you tell me will go any further," he says. "It will be like confession. Unless your friend is planning to blow up the chapel, in which case I might have to advise the bishop."

You risk a watery smile. "Jane was going on about cold feet all night, saying she'd only ever been with Tom." It feels weird telling a priest all this, but it's good to get it out. "And then I got locked out of my room, and I climbed over the balcony, I know, it doesn't make sense, but then . . . but then . . . I saw Jane in Mikey's room. They were together. He's Tom's best man—what were they thinking!" Fresh tears roll down your cheeks.

Father Declan rubs a hand over his stubbled chin. "And people think celibacy is hard. Ah, come here, you *eejit*, nobody's died." He puts an arm around your shoulders. "Do you believe Jane will be happy with this man she's marrying?"

You hesitate, remembering all your doubts. But there's no denying that Tom is steady, decent, and loves Jane. "Yes. Maybe. But what do I do now?"

"It seems to me that you have two options. You can

have it out with Jane. Go to her, tell her what you saw. She may need a friend, someone to talk to. Or you can take the view that there was drink taken, weddings make everyone crazy, and the most sensible thing would be to say nothing."

"But which one is the right thing to do? You're a priest—can't you at least give me a hint?"

Declan slumps slightly, and you look more closely at him. The shadows under his eyes tell a story of long fatigue. "I'm not sure you realize how ironic it is, you asking me for advice on doing the right thing," he sighs. "I'm having a bit of a spiritual crisis myself—that's why I'm lying awake at two in the morning."

"What? Do you mean you don't believe in God anymore?"

He laughs. "No, that's not the problem."

"Is it, um, the celibacy thing?" you venture. Secretly you can't help hoping he's about to renounce his vows.

"Strangely enough, no. Although when a beautiful woman shows up barefoot in a tight dress in my bedroom . . ." He smiles that devastating grin, and your stomach swoops in spite of everything.

You find you're leaning up against his shoulder, so close you can smell the warm, slightly spicy scent of his skin. He goes on, "No, it goes deeper than that. I question my usefulness. These days, I feel like a puppet that gets trotted out whenever someone needs a ritual performed. Meanwhile, surely God would want me fighting real evil: human trafficking, the destruction of the environment, civil war, that sort of thing."

a girl walks into a wedding

He sighs again. "Look, I know I serve a very real purpose when my parishioners are sick or dying, or they need to get something off their chests. But do you know what the real sticking point is for me?"

You're riveted. "Tell me."

"It's the weddings. In the last fifteen years, I've married nearly a thousand couples. And nearly a quarter of them are already divorced or separated. I don't mind that they stand before me, making vows to a God they don't believe in. I don't care that they've been living together. It doesn't even bother me that they probably won't darken the doors of my church again until they want their first child christened."

He turns to you, propping his head on one hand. By now you're loosely holding his other hand. "Go on," you say.

"It's that they make such terribly serious, important vows without thinking through what they're doing. Everyone gets caught up in the wedding fever of dresses and menus and a perfect day, with no clue what it means to share a life together for the next fifty years. I hear couples swearing to love each other 'for better or for worse' without the slightest idea of what 'worse' could mean."

Wow. You hadn't thought of it that way. It's lucky Cee Cee isn't hearing this.

Declan goes on, "And then there's the expense. Young couples going into debt, sometimes filing for divorce before they've even finished paying off the wedding."

He squeezes your hand. "But here I am, going on about myself, and you're in a crisis. Are you feeling any better?"

You'd almost forgotten about Jane, but now your dilemma rushes back in full force. "You're really not going to tell me what I should do?" you say.

"You know I can't. She's your oldest friend—I have a feeling you already know the best way forward. You can't go wrong with the Golden Rule."

"The Golden Rule?"

" 'Do unto others as you would be done by.' Translation: Be kind."

"Thanks." You give him a wobbly smile. "I do feel a bit better."

"Funnily enough, so do I. It seems I'm the one who's done the confessing here." He crinkles his eyes at you again, and then they darken with something stronger than friendly warmth.

He picks up your hand and kisses it very gently, and goose bumps break out all over your skin at the warmth of his lips.

"You'd better go. Or I'm going to have enormous difficulty with that vow of celibacy on top of everything else."

You slip off the bed, and then turn back—you can't stop yourself—and bend to kiss him on those beautifully shaped lips. Your mouths linger together for a long moment, and while you know you've had more passionate kisses, you don't think you've ever had one more tender.

a girl walks into a wedding

You wrench yourself away and out the door. Jane needs you. Your stomach knots. Golden Rule, you repeat. What would be kinder: to confront her right away, or pretend you saw no evil?

❧ If you decide to tell Jane you know, go to page 217.

❧ If you decide to pretend you didn't see anything, go to page 220.

֍ You've decided to tell Jane you know

YOU TAKE A DEEP breath and tap gently on Jane's door, hoping she's back. She snatches open the door, her face streaked with tears.

"I've been so stupid! I've done something terrible!" she wails, pulling you into her room.

Overwhelmed with relief that you won't have to confront her after all, you sit down next to her on the bed and hand her the box of tissues from the dresser.

Jane opens her mouth and the whole story falls out in a tumble of tears. After she returned from the karaoke bar, she was on her way up to her room when she bumped into a very drunk Mikey. They got chatting, she went up to his room to get something, and then . . .

"What the hell were you thinking?" you demand.

"I don't know," she howls. "I've never been with

anyone else, I wasn't sure, I just wanted to see what it was like."

"So you slept with the best man?" you ask, trying your hardest to keep cool, but not succeeding.

She stops midsob and stares at you. "Are you crazy? I didn't sleep with him! I'd never do that. We kissed a bit, and then somehow I touched his dick . . ." Jane wipes her nose with her sleeve.

You're tempted to jam your fingers in your ears, but she goes on, "That was when I came to my senses. It was just so tiny!"

"Really?" This you did not expect.

"I mean chipolata-small! Really, reeeally teeny," Jane says, lifting her little finger and wiggling it around. "To be honest, I didn't know they came that small."

"No way!"

"Yes way. Talk about all bark and no bite. That was when I thought, What the hell am I doing? And I got out of there. Cold feet banished for life. I'm so lucky I found Tom. I know you think he's boring, but he isn't, not really. And even if he is, he's *my* boring."

"Are you going to tell him?" you ask.

"Probably," Jane says, suddenly serious. "Maybe he did something bad at the bachelor party, and then we'll be even."

"You know that's highly unlikely, right?" you say.

"I know. That's why I love him."

Jane looks off into the distance and you catch her expression. You realize, possibly for the first time, just how much she does love him. You put your arms around her.

"It'll all be fine in the end," you promise her. "You just have to remember the Golden Rule."

"Golden Rule?" she asks.

"Be kind."

❧ Go to page 222.

a girl walks into a wedding

ᕈ You've decided to pretend you didn't see anything

Everything is dead quiet as you make your way back to your room. Typically, you discovered that your key was in your jacket pocket all along. You're shattered. Part hangover sneaking up on you, part emotional exhaustion.

There's someone waiting at the end of the hall, sitting with her knees up against her chest, her head down. It's Jane. "Where have you been?" she says, scrambling to her feet. "I have to talk to you!" She shepherds you back to her room.

"I need your help! I've made a terrible mistake!" she says, sinking onto the floor, tears spilling down her cheeks.

"I know," you say, unable to stop yourself. "I saw you with Mikey!"

She looks up at you. "What do you mean, you saw?"

You explain about losing your room key and blundering into Mikey's room, but something stops you from telling her about your encounter with Father Declan.

Jane starts weeping again. "I don't know what I was thinking! I've been having cold feet, and I was worried that I'd never been with anyone else . . ."

"And now that you've been with someone else?" you snap.

"What? Are you nuts? I didn't sleep with him!"

"You didn't?"

"No, absolutely not. It was just kissing, and then I touched his dick . . . and I completely freaked out. I had to get out of there! It just felt so wrong." She scrubs her cheeks with a sodden tissue. "And . . . Mikey was kind of small, too. Very small, in fact!"

"Oh reeaally?" you say, raising your eyebrows. "Tiny, hmm?"

"Like a monkey's finger!" Jane says. You sink onto the floor next to her, and then you both roll around laughing until you can't breathe. Eventually Jane blows her nose and looks at you seriously.

"It turns out that what I already have is just right. I really fucked up. Do you think I should tell Tom?"

"What? That you love his penis? Yes, I think you should tell him that repeatedly for the rest of your lives. The rest we should probably keep to ourselves."

Jane nods dreamily. "I think we're going to live together happily ever after."

"I think so, too," you say, grinning at the thought of Mikey's teeny, tiny, iddle-widdle penis.

👉 Go to page 222.

a girl walks into a wedding

❧ You head back to your room

AS YOU WANDER BACK to your room through the magnificent old manor house, with the birds starting to stir and the dawn light approaching, you hear giggling coming from a room at the end of the hall. You tiptoe toward it.

It's part laundry, part storeroom, the door slightly ajar. You hear more giggling and shuffling, and you peep in.

You see Cat sitting on one of the heavy-duty washing machines, with Lisa standing between her legs. They're kissing passionately, their eyes closed. Lisa is holding Cat's face and Cat's fingers are trailing down Lisa's spine. You tiptoe away, dazed and shaking your head. Is everyone getting it on tonight?

Back in your room, you think about everything you've seen. Between the wild karaoke, catching Jane with Mikey, and getting to know Declan a little better, it's been a whirlwind evening. And you don't even know how to begin processing what you've just seen in the laundry room.

Poor Bruno, even though you can't stand him, you feel a little sorry for him. And then, as you sink onto your bed, you can't help thinking about Declan. Father Declan. No, you prefer him as just Declan.

You shake off the thought of that lilting accent and that sexy mouth. You're going straight to hell at this rate. And the weekend has hardly begun. It's the rehearsal dinner tomorrow tonight—no, wait, it's already tomorrow.

But what will you do for the day? You need to get out of the hotel, that's for sure, or Cee Cee will rope you into wedding-planning hell. Jane is spending the day with Aunt Lauren, so she won't need you. You could sleep late and then maybe head over to the spa for a bikini wax. Except those are always so painful—a massage would be a lot more relaxing. You yawn—you'll decide when you wake up.

ᔰ To go for a wax, go to page 224.

ᔰ To get a massage, go to page 225.

You've gone for a wax at the spa

YOU SIP GRATEFULLY AT your glass of ice-cold lemon-and-mint water as you wait for the beauty therapist. It's a shame you're here for a bikini wax and not something a little less excruciating. But you took a hard look at what was going on downstairs before you got in the shower this morning and decided your George Bush was starting to look like Donald Trump.

"I am so sorry," drawls Olga, the glamazon beautician, clopping in on high heels. "No vaxing this veekend—the heating machine caught on fire. But ve have a cancellation, if you vant a massage instead."

If you have a massage, go to page 225.

If you head back to the hotel, go to page 233.

❧ You're getting a massage

 YOU LIE ON YOUR stomach on the massage table, naked under a warm, fluffy towel. The door opens and a man steps in.

"Hello," he says, smiling politely. "I'm Claud."

You smile and greet him back. You've never had a male massage therapist before, but you're quite looking forward to it. It feels like a modern and mature thing to do. Claud is slim, with the kind of complexion that suggests a lifetime of eating wheatgrass and vitamin smoothies. His arms are muscled in a way that makes you think he's probably a yoga buff, too.

He opens a bottle and the smell of pine and eucalyptus fills the room. Through the hole in the massage table you can see Claud's legs, clad in a pair of white linen trousers, as he moves around the table.

"So, just tell me if the pressure is too soft, or too hard, okay?" he says, and you nod as you feel his fingers on your back, the oil warm on your skin, his fingers soft, but hard and probing at the same time. You breathe out, sighing with pleasure as he gets to work on the knotted muscles in your neck and shoulders. Then he works down either side of your spine in long, even strokes.

You feel his fingers roving lower and lower down your back, and then he folds the towel down farther, so that the top of your bottom is exposed to his fingers, which are working their magic, kneading, stroking, and rubbing away every single tension you ever had. As his fingers massage the tops of your buttocks, you feel your pussy responding, which takes you by surprise. You can't remember ever feeling turned on during a massage before. You wonder if it's because your masseur is such a good-looking guy, or whether it's his fingers, which should be insured for billions.

"If you could turn over now," Claud says, laying a fresh, warm towel over you so that you can turn without flashing your naked body. Then he pours more oil into his hands and gets to work on your front. You feel those clever fingers on your shoulders, and then he drops them down, so he's massaging the top of your chest.

You murmur a little and open your legs slightly underneath the towel. He's standing just to your right, and your head is exactly at waist height. You can even see the shape of his cock through the light linen of his trousers. Is that an erection, or is it simply the way the light is falling?

As his fingers rub across your chest, you wonder if you'd want him to take things further. And would that cost extra, or is it simply a win-win situation for everyone? And if you did want a happy ending, how would you let your masseur know? Is there some sort of code word for this kind of thing?

- ❧ If you want to say something suggestive, go to page 228.

- ❧ If that is most definitely a bad idea, go to page 230.

❧ You propose a happy ending

YOU FEEL BOLD. PROPPING yourself up on your elbows, you flutter your lashes at Claud. "Any chance of a happy ending?"

"What the—!" Claud snatches his hands away and backs off.

"I'm sorry, for a second I thought you were . . . I thought this was . . ." Your mouth has gone dry.

"How dare you? I'm going to have to ask you to leave!" Claud shouts.

"Shh . . . shhhh . . ." you say, worried someone might hear him. "I'm so sorry, I didn't mean . . . it was a misunderstanding . . . can't we just pretend it didn't happen?"

"What kind of establishment do you think this is? And what kind of masseur do you think I am? I trained in Sweden, you know! You should be ashamed of yourself!" He reaches for a tissue and angrily wipes the oil from his fingers.

"Wait," you call as he storms out the door. "I'm sorry! Don't go! I've still got fifteen minutes left!"

❧ You're massaged (more or less) and ready
   for the rehearsal dinner. Go to page 233.

❧ You don't propose anything improper

EVEN IF YOU REALLY wanted to say something suggestive, you couldn't possibly be that forward. You keep your mouth shut as Claud begins to work on your legs. He kneads at your ankles and then up your shins, squeezing at your calves, then working at the skin above your knees with strong, agile fingers. Next he moves up your thighs slowly, first one and then the other, stroking at the muscles, applying just the right amount of pressure.

You can feel your pussy pulsing under the shield of the towel, his fingers just inches away from it. You have to concentrate to stop yourself from shifting your hips to force him to touch you higher. You imagine his long, deft fingers straying from their course, slipping under the towel, slipping inside you one by one, and at the thought of it, a little moan escapes you.

"Does that hurt?" Claud asks, stopping what he's doing.

You have to clear your throat. "No, it's perfect," you say huskily and he continues his fingers' journey, using his thumbs like rollers against your skin.

"I'm afraid that's time," Claud finally says, and you open your eyes slowly, feeling disappointment surge through your body. You're not at all ready for this to be over.

"Be careful not to get up too fast, you may feel light-headed," Claud says from above you. "And take your time getting dressed. Come out whenever you're ready; there's no hurry." Then he leaves you alone in the dim light of the treatment room.

You remain on your back, breathing slowly, every muscle relaxed and at ease, but every nerve ending alert. You stroke your hand along your stomach, feeling the slip and slide of the oil on your skin. Then you trail your other hand down your side and over your hip, tossing the towel to the floor. You lay your palm over your mound and apply the slightest pressure. You roll your hips a little, aware that you don't have all that much time.

You squeeze your thighs together and contract your pussy, and it sends sharp waves of need shooting through your body. Then you slip your hand between your soaking wet pussy lips, your fingers sliding between hot skin. You find your clit with your middle finger and push down on it, then slip that finger farther down your slit, then up again, first flicking it over your clit, then scissoring your clit between two fingers, and you have to stop yourself from crying out. You slip two fingers into your pussy, the walls of it hot and eager, sucking you inside. You grind your hips up to push against the top of your palm, which is pressed down on your clit, then slip a third finger inside yourself. You raise and spread your legs so that you can move your fingers inside you, until at last your orgasm begins to explode around you with a rare intensity. Your clit feels on fire as you pulse your palm down on it, every feeling amplified as your body spasms, your eyes squeezed shut.

As the waves of intense pleasure finally recede, you release your fingers and lie still until your body calms. Then you stretch luxuriously and slip off the table to find your clothes. You've never felt more relaxed.

❧ Now you're ready for the rehearsal dinner.
Go to page 233.

Helena L. Paige

❧ It's the night of the rehearsal dinner

You step onto your hotel balcony in your bra and panties, wiggling your fingers in front of you as you wait for your nail polish to dry. Your room has a view out over the formal rose garden, and at this time of day, the scent of the blooms is so strong, it's almost like smoke. The distant lake looks gilded, along with the tops of the trees.

"Ahem."

Startled, you turn to see Bruno sitting on the balcony next to yours, dressed for dinner, with a drink in his hand and his feet up on the balcony wall. You shoot into your room, where you reach for a long T-shirt and slip it on, careful not to smudge your nails. Then you go back outside.

"I didn't think there'd be anyone out here," you say, cheeks burning.

"No worries, Stinky," Bruno says with an evil grin.

"My name is not Stinky! Why do you always have to be such a jerk?"

"But I've always called you Stinky," he says, surprised. "It's a term of endearment."

"No, it's not. It's a term of assholeism."

"I didn't realize you didn't like it."

"How could you not realize that? What woman wants to be called Stinky?"

Bruno's face drops. You flash back to Cat and Lisa getting hot and heavy last night, and you suddenly feel a little bad for him.

"I'm sorry," he says. "You're right, we're not eleven anymore, it's not appropriate. I won't do it again."

You nod, feeling silly for making such a fuss over it. "We got up to some crazy stuff back then, didn't we?"

"The massacre of the G.I. Joes will never be forgotten."

"Just getting revenge. You know, for stuff that would land you in a young offenders' institution these days. Hair-burning. Assault with a deadly cow pie. That kind of thing."

"Look, I suppose I should explain. When we were kids, I always thought you were sort of awesome. I had a little crush on you, and I guess the only way I knew how to deal with it was to pick on you."

"You did not!" you say.

"Did too!" he says, and you both laugh.

"Really? You mean it? All those years ago, you liked me?"

"Yup." His gaze holds yours and you can't look away.

In fact, you don't want to. You want to hear more about this crush—it certainly shakes up your memories of Bruno as a boy.

"Uncle Bruno! Uncle Bruno! Knuckle Bronko!" Domino are panting across the lawn after their kids, who are racing ahead of them.

"To be continued," Bruno says as he leaps over the balcony with surprisingly athletic ease, and falls to his knees on the grass, not caring that he's ruining his smart trousers. The children climb on top of him for piggyback rides up and down the lawn. You can't help smiling.

YOU'RE ABOUT TO LEAVE the room for the rehearsal dinner, when there's a knock on the door and Jane enters. You saw her briefly when you returned from the spa—Aunt Lauren was whisking her away for a French manicure and an expensive boozy lunch—but she sent you a text, telling you not to worry about her.

You give her a hug. "How are you feeling?"

"Still a bit hungover, but Aunt Lauren has been feeding me Bloody Marys all day. Listen . . . I've decided that telling Tom about last night will only hurt him. I know for sure now that I want to be with him. Does that make me a coward?"

The delectable Father Declan's words come back to you. "No. It makes you kind. Everyone can have a moment of madness. And Mikey is hardly likely to say anything, is he?"

Jane sighs. "No way. We had a chat after breakfast. He feels awful, too."

You find that a little hard to believe, but decide to keep it to yourself. "If you think about it, in a twisted way, Mikey's done you a favor. If it wasn't for his teeny monkey penis you might still be having doubts about Tom."

Jane gives a half chuckle. "This is going to sound crazy, but until last night, I had no idea they could be so tiny! And did you know that not all penises are bendy? I just assumed they were all like Tom's."

You flash back to your night with the pilot, and his oddly bent penis. But this isn't the time or the place to mention your own escapades. "Too much information! Seriously, Jane, I'm so glad you and Tom are back on track."

"It's getting late, I'd better get going. Thanks for being there for me. And not judging me." Jane hugs you again and hurries off. If nothing else, the entire episode has quelled your nagging doubts about whether Tom is the best guy for her. It's clear that she'd fall apart without him.

As you make your way to the rehearsal dinner, you decide that your next duty is to have a word with Lisa about her extracurricular activities last night.

"Hello again." You turn to see the DJ exiting his room, looking hot enough to melt the iceberg that sank the *Titanic*. "I looked for you last night," he says. "Thought you might have liked a nightcap."

Hmm, why are you always in the wrong place at the

wrong time? This man definitely makes your pulse race a little faster.

"How about a rain check?" you ask.

"Deal," he says.

OF COURSE, CEE CEE has planned the rehearsal dinner with military precision. From the dress code (smart) to the seating arrangements (each place adorned with a handcrafted name card in gold-inked calligraphy), and even the location—an elegant function room that's been partitioned so that it fits just one long, narrow table.

You wander around the table, looking for your seat. It's an intimate affair, just family and close friends. You find your place—the card to your left says Lisa and the one to your right, Cee Cee.

"Over here," you call when Lisa walks in, rocking a fitted tuxedo, with excessively high luminous pink heels that match her hair. You're glad she's sitting next to you—it'll give you a chance to interrogate her about seeing her sucking face, and who knows what else, with the bride's brother's girlfriend.

Your stomach flutters as Father Declan sits across from you. How is it possible that he gets better-looking every time you see him? You greet each other warmly, and then Bruno and Cat take their places to his right. You can't miss the smoldering looks passing between Cat and Lisa.

You whisper in Lisa's ear, "I know what you did last night."

"Jesus, fuck," Lisa bursts out.

"We can talk about it later," you say.

"No, look!" You follow her gaze and almost fall off your chair. It's the pilot from two nights ago. He's walking across the room toward you. You struggle to breathe. What's he doing here? Has he been stalking you?

"Dad!" Tom says, pumping the pilot's fist and giving him a hug.

Suddenly it all falls into place. The bent penis—like father, like son. You've slept with the father of the groom. You cover your face with your purse. Lisa is still gaping beside you, and then she bursts into snorts of laughter.

"Don't say a word! I've got dirt on you from last night," you snap.

Tom walks his dad around the table, introducing him. Shit, shit, shit, you think as he gets closer.

When the pilot sees you, he does a double take. "It's you!" he says, and then he spots Lisa. "And you!"

"You know each other?" Tom says, baffled, but polite. "But how—"

"We met the other night," you say, aware that your voice is unusually high.

"Yes, you could say she *knows* him, in a sense," Lisa says, and you kick her hard under the table.

Jane calls Tom to join her, and shooting you and his dad (his *dad*, oh god) a last puzzled glance, he leaves. Lisa pinches you playfully and turns to talk to Cat, leaving you alone with Mr. Bruce Willis.

"So you're Tom's dad!" you say, overly bright.

"That I am, and your connection is . . . ?"

"Bride's best friend," you say. You're sure your face is scarlet.

"Small world," he says.

"So small!"

"Tiny."

You rattle your brain for something to say. "How come I haven't seen you . . . um . . . around here? At this hotel, I mean."

"They were full. That's why I'm staying at the other one."

"Right."

"I missed you the other morning," he says, leaning forward, his voice intimate.

You tug at the neckline of your dress, which suddenly feels too tight.

"Jack!" Aunt Lauren swoops down on the pair of you in a swathe of expensive perfume, and wraps her arms around him. Perhaps a Vivienne Westwood ball gown is a little over-the-top for a rehearsal dinner, but that's Aunt Lauren for you.

"Hello, Lauren," the pilot says, kissing her on the cheek.

"How fabulous to see you again—it's been far too long, stranger," she purrs. "I see we're sitting next to each other, what a lovely surprise!" She winks at you in a way that makes you think it's not really a surprise to her at all.

She loops her arm through his. "Shall we sit down? What say we try and make that ex-wife of yours a little jealous?"

Jack gives you a helpless look as Aunt Lauren drags him away.

"Son of a bitch," you whisper to Lisa as she turns to you again. "Of all the men in the vicinity this weekend, why did I have to sleep with Tom's dad? This is all your fault, you know. You were the one who saw him first!"

"Tom's dad or not, he's still hot!" Lisa says.

You check him out surreptitiously, sitting at the opposite end of the table to Tom's mother and her boyfriend. Aunt Lauren is murmuring in his ear, her hand on his arm. Clearly you and Lisa aren't the only ones who think he's hot.

Okay, you've made it through the first five minutes of dinner, you think, and it's been excruciating. You reach for your wineglass: Only two and a half hours left to go.

You survey the rest of the table. There's so much electricity zinging between Lisa and Cat, you can't believe that nobody else at the table has noticed. You glance at Bruno, but he seems blissfully unaware, and when he catches you glancing at him, he smiles sweetly. He must feel bad about the earful you gave him earlier, you think. But you're glad to have gotten it off your chest. The two of you might even end up friends at this rate.

A cell phone rings, and you're aware of Jack taking a call. Then you see him getting up and saying something to Tom.

"I'm afraid I have to leave," he says to the table, and your eyes meet briefly.

"Pilot emergency?" Aunt Lauren asks.

"Something like that. But I'll see you all tomorrow

at the wedding." He glances at you again, then leaves. You wonder if that call was a ruse to save you both from further embarrassment, and you sit back, relieved and at the same time, slightly disappointed. But it's for the best. If you'd known he was Tom's dad, you definitely wouldn't have hooked up with him.

You turn your attention back to Father Declan. He really is exceptionally attractive, especially tonight, in an all-black suit. Smoking hot is the only way to put it. And after your heart-to-heart last night, you feel connected to him. Your conversation was almost more intimate than if you'd screwed each other senseless. He's making Noe laugh, his face crinkling in that devastating smile, but he still has those shadows under his eyes.

Halfway through the main course, an extremely complicated risotto, you feel a foot against yours under the table. At first it's just a bump, but the next time you feel it, there's more to it. You freeze, a forkful of sun-dried tomato halfway to your mouth. You look around. There's Noe, who's busy dicing up food and feeding it to her kids, seated next to Declan, who is seated beside Bruno, who's in the middle of an intense conversation with Lisa, Cat, and Aunt Lauren. As you contemplate whose foot it might be, you catch Declan's eye, and he smiles.

Good god, it's him! He's the one playing footsie with you under the table! You knew you hadn't been imagining the chemistry between you last night. Heat surges through your body from the tips of your toes to the edges of your earlobes. He smiles at you again, his eyes creasing at the corners, then goes back to his conversation with Jane's mom, a few seats down from you.

You feel his foot move again. It briefly rubs over your ankle, then withdraws. You hold your breath and push your fork around your plate, too aroused to eat anything more. You wait for the sensation of his foot against yours again, wondering if maybe you imagined it. But no, it definitely happened, your foot is still burning where he touched you. Declan catches your eye again, and this time he winks, and that's all the confirmation you need. You slip your foot out of your shoe, and stretch your leg forward until it finds its mark, and you feel the crook of an ankle under your toes. Then you lift your foot slowly, slowly up his leg.

Declan drops his fork onto his plate with a clatter and starts coughing. You drop your foot. Noe turns to him and whacks him on the back until his coughing fit passes, before going back to wrangling Paris or Penang or Perth, who's trying to shove a chicken leg (in a miso, ginger, and sesame crust) into her water glass.

Declan reaches for his wine and shoots you a surprised look. You continue playing with your food, your face innocent, and return your foot to his calf, this time running your foot all the way up his leg, then down again, and then up one last time, before lodging your foot in his crotch, pleasantly surprised by the solid hardness you find there.

You can tell that Declan is trying desperately to remain outwardly calm. He lays his napkin over his lap just as Jane's mom asks him about the new organist at their home parish.

As the waitress clears plates, Declan excuses himself. You wait a few minutes, then, unable to remain burning in your seat any longer, you follow him.

You bump into him just outside the room and he grasps you by the hand and pulls you into an empty and darkened function room, a narrow space filled with spare tables and chairs and a sofa against the window. He leads you into a corner, and you can't tell if it's anger or desire you see storming in his eyes.

He tries to start three different sentences and then gives up, groaning as he folds you into his arms. You can feel his heart banging away against your chest.

"What am I going to do with you?" he says, dropping a kiss onto your hair. You wriggle against him, desperate for more, tipping your face up to him. He gazes intently into your eyes, but makes no move to kiss you.

You can't bear it. You stand on tiptoe and press your mouth against his. For a long minute, he doesn't respond. And then, with a sound of satisfaction, his mouth opens against yours. You almost swoon with desire and relief, luxuriating in the softness and warmth of his mouth before you tentatively slide your tongue against his. Slowly, agonizingly slowly, he responds, meeting you halfway, shifting his head so that his stubble rasps against your face. You clutch the back of his neck, rocking your hips against him, and however conflicted he may feel emotionally, his erection is in no doubt whatsoever.

And then it's like a dam breaking, he's all over you, kissing you frantically, sliding his hands down to your bottom and holding you against him so hard, he's almost rough.

You tumble onto the sofa, panting, and he clutches you, his face creased as if close to tears. He shuts his eyes and leans his forehead against yours. You move a fingertip along his lips, and then kiss him along his jaw-line, slowly working your way down the side of his neck, inhaling the rich, masculine smell of him as you go.

"What are we doing?" he whispers.

"You started it," you say.

"I did?"

"Yes!" You're indignant. "What was all that footsie under the table?"

"I didn't start it—that was you!"

If it wasn't Declan's foot, then whose was it? The realization dawns: It could only have been Bruno. You flash back to your conversation earlier on the balcony, and the glances he was giving you across the table this evening. But that doesn't change how you're feeling now.

"I'm sorry. I know it's not allowed, but I've never wanted anyone more," you say.

"Me neither. I just wish it wasn't so complicated."

❧ If it's too complicated to be with him, go to page 245.

❧ If you want to be with him even though it's complicated, go to page 249.

It's too complicated

"I GET IT," YOU say. "I don't want to get it, but I get it."

"Oh, the hell with it," he says, and leans toward you again, clasping your head with both hands and kissing you desperately, deeply, his tongue rolling over yours, a drowning man clinging to a raft. This time it's you who pulls away, after long minutes of pure ecstasy. It takes every grain of willpower you have, and you know how much you're going to regret it later, but you can't go through with this: There's too much at stake.

"Declan, I can't," you say, holding both his hands. "It's not that I don't want to, I want to more than anything in the world right now, but I can't be responsible for this. It's too big a thing."

You both stay where you are on the sofa, your faces almost touching, just breathing for a minute. Then he rests his fingertips on your cheeks, and kisses you very gently on the lips.

"I can't stay," he says.

"What do you mean?" you stutter.

"I can't stay and go through with this wedding. It would make me the worst kind of hypocrite, and I know you understand why. This"—he looks at you—"has just brought everything to a head."

"Wait," you say, grabbing hold of his arms. "You can't leave now, Jane's wedding is in the morning." You feel the breath leaving your body. You can't be responsible for Jane's priest going AWOL. Cee Cee will literally kill you.

"I'm sorry. But I have to leave."

"No! Please, just think about it! What would Jesus do? Ask yourself that. He would definitely stay and marry Jane!"

Declan laughs. "I wish I'd met you twenty years ago. Let me tell you, Jesus wouldn't be staying in a joint like this. He'd probably be off chucking bankers out of the temple of Mammon somewhere." He kisses the tip of your nose. "Will you tell them I've left?" he says. "And tell Jane I wish her well. I hope she and her fella go the distance."

"Wait!" you call as he gets up, still holding your hand. "Where are you going?"

You see his teeth shining in the gloom of the room. "I'm off to join Greenpeace. After that, who knows? You take the best care of yourself." He kisses your hand, then he's gone.

Shit. What are you going to tell Jane? Eventually you wobble back to the private dining room to face the firing squad—although Cee Cee strikes you as more of a stabber.

You wave away your untouched chocolate mousse, adorned with vanilla swirls and a nest of spun sugar— you missed an entire course while you were out un-priesting the priest. Someone taps on a wineglass and everyone quiets down. Lisa shoots you a worried glance, and Bruno is staring at you. You're not sure how you missed it before—the intent behind his glances is obvious.

"Where's Father Declan?" Jane's mom asks, looking around.

You clear your throat. "He asked me to make his ex-cuses. He had to go up to his room to . . . to deal with a parish matter." This isn't the kind of news you break in front of a crowd, not even one that's just had a good meal and plenty of wine.

After the speeches, you pull Jane and Lisa to one side. "I need to tell you something," you start.

"What is it?" Jane says, panic filling her eyes. She knows your guilty face too well.

"Declan didn't just leave to go to his room."

"Oh, fuck! What have you done now?" Lisa says, getting it immediately.

"What do you mean?" Jane asks, a little slower on the uptake.

"He had to leave," you stammer, "because he's having a . . . a . . . crisis of faith."

"You dirty—" Lisa starts, covering her mouth. "You fucking legend!" She holds her hand up for a high five, which you ignore.

"No, it's not like that!" you protest.

"You fucked my priest, and now he's left?" Jane says a little too loudly, making heads turn.

"I didn't fuck him!" you hiss. "We just kissed a bit. I couldn't help it. I mean, have you *looked* at the guy? He's a fucking god!"

"Not quite, he just works for one," Lisa says. "Which makes what you've done worse, if you think about it."

"You're not helping!" you say, exasperated.

"You broke this, you'd better fix it!" Jane says, prodding you in the chest with a pointy, manicured, panicked-bride finger.

❧ Who's going to perform the ceremony now?
   Go to page 257.

Helena L. Paige

🙠 You want to be with him even though it's complicated

"I UNDERSTAND, IT'S COMPLICATED," you say, nodding earnestly.

"Oh, the hell with complicated," he says, and launches himself back at you. Your mouths crush together and you close your eyes and sink into the warmth of him. Which you realize is all you've wanted to do since you met him.

You run your hands tentatively across his chest, and he groans into your mouth at your touch. You pop open a couple of buttons so you can feel his skin against your fingertips. The enormity of what you're doing makes you almost tearful and even hungrier for him. At last you feel his fingers quivering as he touches you, cupping your shoulders. You reach up and slide the strap of your dress off your shoulder, and he runs his mouth down your neck, and then stops to kiss your shoulder. Then, very gently, he cradles your breast in his hand.

"It's been a very long time," he says quietly.

"It's okay," you say. You press him back on the sofa, and carefully lower yourself onto his lap, straddling him, afraid to rush him. He brings both hands up to the edge of your dress, and in the dim light, you can see them trembling. You help him peel the fabric away, and he slides his palms around your breasts, his thumbs slowly stroking against your nipples, which are as hard as diamonds. He caresses your breasts for a long time, before lowering his head. You clasp the back of his head gently as he drops his mouth onto the tender skin of your breasts. You gasp as he finds first one nipple, and then the other, and for a long time, he worships you with his mouth. At last you tug his head back up, and you kiss with such intensity, you're amazed you don't burst into flames.

You can't bear the waiting any longer, and you reach for his buckle and fumble with it, your hands shaking from all the adrenaline rushing through your body. You carefully release his button and zipper and reach for his cock, which is standing at attention—it's been waiting years for your touch. He drops his head back into your neck and nuzzles there, breathing deeply as you wrap your hand around his shaft. He groans again and tilts his head backward. Then he covers your hand with his, halting it for a moment, the feeling clearly too intense for him. So you hold his pulsating cock still in your hand while he breathes slowly through what he's feeling. You're thrilled at the effect you're having on him, but his need is making your own hunger unbearable.

Helena L. Paige

"My purse," you whisper, and he reaches for it next to you, fumbling with the catch. A woman's purse is an entirely foreign object to him. You take it from him and snap it open, feeling in the side pocket for the emergency condom you keep in there. You hate to break away from him, but you have to get your soaked panties off, so you stand up for a second to strip them off. Then you clamber astride him once more, one arm around his neck, as you rip at the condom wrapper.

You kiss him softly, then slip the condom over his cock. It's so hard, you're afraid he might explode before you can even get him inside you, which is what you really need. Urgently. Right now. "Coming, ready or not," you say in his ear, as you settle yourself over his cock, lodging the tip between your wet pussy lips, and then sinking slowly down. He cries out and clutches at your back.

He feels huge thrusting up inside you, and you try to hold still, to make the moment last as long as you can, kissing his forehead, but Declan can't hold on for a second longer, and he comes silently, his shoulders heaving under your fingertips. You wrap your arms around him and rest your cheek against his.

When you finally open your eyes, the room feels different—the light has changed. Declan remains oblivious to the world, his head dropped into the hollow of your collarbone. You feel a trickle of sweat—or could it be a tear?—running down his cheek and falling onto your skin.

At last you shift off him, and as you turn, you see

Jane and her mom, standing at the other end of the room, their mouths gaping, both with their arms full of gifts. Panicked, you prod at Declan, and push down your dress.

Declan goes pale when he sees them. "Oh, feck," he mumbles, pulling up his zipper. Lisa and Cee Cee appear behind Jane and her mom, their hands also full of beautifully wrapped gifts. There's an almighty smash as one of the boxes tumbles out of Cee Cee's arms and crashes to the floor.

Jane is rigid with horror.

"Fuck me!" Lisa says. "I wondered where you'd got to. Bless you, Father, for you have sinned!"

Jane's mom reels back a couple of paces and sits down on one of the stacked chairs, and Cee Cee follows suit. The room goes deathly quiet. The wedding etiquette guides don't cover this scenario.

Declan clears his throat as he buttons up his shirt. "Jane, I'm afraid I don't think I'm going to be able to marry you tomorrow."

"You think?" Lisa says.

Jane just gapes, her mouth opening and closing.

"It's probably best if I leave," Declan says. "I am so very sorry for all the inconvenience." Then he turns toward you and kisses you, stroking your cheek delicately with his thumb before walking out of the room, his head down.

"See you at church next Sunday," Jane's mom calls after him in a robotic, overly polite voice.

"Mom!" Jane snaps. "I highly doubt it!"

"Jane, I am SO sorry," you say.

"I did NOT see that coming," Cee Cee says, finally finding her voice.

Unable to hold it in anymore, Lisa bursts out laughing, huge guffaws racking her body.

"Shit," says Jane. "Who the hell is going to marry me and Tom now?" She smacks Lisa's arm. "Stop laughing, it's not funny."

Then she turns on you. "I am supposed to be getting married in less than twelve hours. Father Declan has known me since I was a girl. And you—you've managed to sabotage the whole thing. Of all the guys you had to screw, why did you have to go after my priest?"

Her mom and Cee Cee are nodding, their faces stern. You're in serious trouble. "Jane—" you start.

But it's too late, her voice is rising to a shriek. "You've ruined my wedding! I want you to leave. Now!"

"But—" you fumble. Other people are starting to filter into the room, drawn by the shouting, but Jane is in one of her rare full-blown tempers. Even Lisa is looking nervous. Jane rounds on the crowd. "She fucked the priest, and now he's walked out, and I don't know how I'm supposed to get married tomorrow." She bursts into tears and storms out. Tom shoots you an appalled look before hurrying after her.

You can feel the waves of disapproval coming at you, and you quail. "I'm so sorry." Domino pull their children away as if you have a communicable disease as you slink past them and head for your room, jangling with shock.

You throw your clothes into your bag, but leave the Dress of Salmon Shame behind—the one tiny silver lining of this entire fiasco is that you won't have to wear it tomorrow.

Just as you're gathering up your toiletries in the bathroom, you hear a knock on the bedroom door. You can't help a little flare of hope—has Declan come back?

Jane hurries into the room, her face still tearstained. You stare at each other for a long minute, then you both blurt out, "I'm sorry!" at the same moment, and the next thing you're hugging, then breaking apart to fumble for tissues and blow your noses.

"Jane, I really am sorry. I didn't plan for any of this to happen. And I want you to know, I wasn't just experimenting—for the novelty value. I felt a real connection with Declan."

"I'm so sorry for shouting at you to leave like that! It was the shock, and a dose of bridezilla nerves, too. I'm really disappointed Father Declan won't be marrying us tomorrow, but Cee Cee is already hunting down a replacement."

"She does thrive on a crisis." You both smile shakily.

Jane reaches for your hand. "I do actually want you to stay."

"That means a lot—thank you. And I wish I could. But it's just going to be too embarrassing. There'll be an atmosphere and gossip, and I don't want to do anything more to spoil your wedding day. It would probably be best for everyone if I left quietly, don't you think?"

"You may be right," sighs Jane. "I'll miss you, though.

And what about Father Declan—will you be seeing him again? God, it feels weird even asking!"

"I don't know if there's any chance of a future for us. The situation isn't exactly normal. But even if we never cross paths again, I can't regret what we did. It was really beautiful. Even if it did throw a wrench in your wedding works."

"That's putting it mildly!" Jane hugs you again, fiercely. "Good luck," she says.

"You too. Have a wonderful wedding, and give Tom my best. Tell your parents I'll write them, to apologize."

After a last round of good-bye hugs, you creep down to reception and ask the night manager to call you a taxi.

"I just did, for the other gentleman, the priest," she says, raising a thinly plucked eyebrow.

Declan! You drag your bag out the front doors and spot a rangy figure pacing up and down on the lawn.

"It's at times like this I wish I still smoked," he says as you approach. "What are you doing out here?"

"I thought it would be best if I left. Otherwise I really am going to be a bad fairy at the feast tomorrow." Your voice wobbles.

He wraps his arms around you. "Two orphans in the storm. Now what?"

It's a relief to lean against him. "I'm open to any bright ideas."

Declan pulls back to look at your face. "I've been wearing out my shoes, trying to pluck up the courage to go looking for you, and here you are."

255

He pauses, and his face twists. "Look, I have to be honest. I am not exactly a good prospect right now. I have no idea what my future holds other than a lot of complications. But this I do know. I'm not leaving without you."

You feel a smile blooming at his words. "I'm not expecting any declarations or promises. But while we're together, at least we can do this."

You stand on tiptoe to kiss him as a spatter of gravel announces the arrival of the taxi.

Declan rests his hands on your shoulders, and his eyes crinkle. "All right. Shall we go, then?" He hurls both your bags into the back and then helps you get into the cab.

"It looks like this is the beginning of the end. Or the end of the beginning. Or something," he says.

You curl against him and tug his face down to yours, searching for his mouth. "Or something," you say. And lose yourself in kissing and being kissed as the taxi purrs along the road.

The End

> ✎ You need to find someone to perform
> Jane's wedding ceremony

"PASS THE HONEY, PLEASE."

Cee Cee glares at you, ignoring your request. It's not the end of the world that she's not talking to you over breakfast. At least Jane and Lisa are, and they're the ones who really matter.

And you're not completely persona non grata with everyone else at the wedding, either: Aunt Lauren thinks you're a legend, and Noe thinks you're a goddess. As a kind of penance (and to avoid Jane's furious parents), you offered to put the kids to bed after the rehearsal dinner. You ended up helping them make a miniature bow tie and tux bib for Yodabell the pet rat, and staging a three-way wedding between it, Sunrise Barbie, and Malibu Ken, which went some way toward taking your mind off the Declan debacle and his hasty departure.

"I've been on the phone most of the night. I called every wedding venue in a thirty-mile radius," you say.

"Good. You broke it, you fix it!" Cee Cee snaps. She's grumpy, but she loves this. Nobody shines more than Cee Cee during a wedding crisis.

"I found out that there are nine weddings today in this area. Six of them are at the same time as ours, which leaves three possible licensed marriage officiants. I've spoken to two of them—they're available and willing to help us, and I still need to talk to the third. So at least we have options."

"Oh, thank goodness," Jane says, slumping back in her seat, the massive curlers in her hair bobbing. "I knew everything was going to be okay."

Cee Cee glances at her watch and gets up. "Jane, the makeup team is arriving any second. We'd better go."

"Wait, what about choosing a marriage officiant?" you say as Cee Cee whisks Jane away.

"You choose one," Jane says, over her shoulder.

"Wait!"

"Just make sure you don't want to jump whoever you pick!" Jane calls as she and Cee Cee disappear.

"Dammit!" you say to Lisa once they've gone.

"What?" she says.

"There's a small glitch I didn't have a chance to mention."

"What?"

"Of the ones who are available, we have an Elvis impersonator. And then there's a new age guru. And I'm still waiting to hear back from a justice of the peace."

"Classic!" Lisa hoots. "Doesn't anybody get married normally anymore?"

"Beggars can't be choosers," you say, chewing at your nails.

❧ If you pick the Elvis impersonator marriage officiant, go to page 260.

❧ If you choose the justice of the peace, go to page 294.

❧ If you choose the new age marriage officiant, go to page 305.

a girl walks into a wedding

∞ You pick the Elvis impersonator

CEE CEE FLUTTERS AROUND Jane, adjusting her skirt. Then Mr. B. holds out his arm to his daughter, and she takes it with a smile. You can't believe how beautiful she looks. You have a lump in your throat, but that might just be from nerves.

Cee Cee kneels in front of the flower girls and gives them one last set of instructions. Tokyo is sulking because Yodabell the rat has been banished to his cage at the back of the church. Paris starts crying because she's already dumped her basket of rose petals on Manhattan's head, but Cee Cee quickly takes a handful of petals out of each of the girls' baskets to replenish hers, and the crisis is averted just as Elvis lifts his guitar and starts singing, "Fools Rush In." And that's the bridesmaids' cue to start walking down the aisle.

You have to admit that as far as Elvis impersonators go, you're getting your money's worth. The replacement "priest" is wearing an electric-blue Elvis jumpsuit, decorated from head to toe in shiny rhinestones. He has huge bouffant hair, and he's wearing a pair of giant white sunglasses. Tom is doing his best to keep a straight face and next to him, Mikey is shaking with silent laughter.

Jane catches her first glimpse of Elvis as she walks down the aisle and pauses to shoot you a glare. If looks could kill, you'd be speared through the heart. You mouth "I'm sorry!" but she's already breaking into a smile as she sees Tom waiting at the altar.

Your heart melts as Jane walks toward Tom. Unfortunately you'll never be able to look at Tom again without thinking about his dad and that bendy penis. What are the chances? Of all the guys in all the wedding villages in all the world, the one you decide to hook up with, on your first-ever one-night stand, turns out to be your best friend's about-to-be-husband's dad. You do a sweep of Tom's side of the church—you can't miss his dad's clean-shaven head in the crowd, and your tummy does a little sex-memory flip. He turns to watch Jane walk down the aisle and spots you. He's handsome in a fitted black Armani suit and a thin black tie, and he smiles at you, which makes your tummy flip again.

Elvis breaks into song at every opportunity he gets. So there's a rousing rendition of "Love Me Tender" in place of a sermon. And he does the wedding vows in song as Jane's mom pats tears from her cheeks.

"If anyone sees any good reason why these two should not be wed, speak now or forever hold your peace," Elvis croons.

a girl walks into a wedding

You look around, holding your breath. But nobody says a word.

"Then by the powers vested in me by the State of Graceland, I now pronounce you husband and uh-huh-huh . . . wife. You may kiss the bride."

Elvis whips his guitar around to the front of his body and launches into a lively and inappropriate version of "Hound Dog," complete with wild pelvic rotations.

Domino cover their children's eyes with their hands.

Tom and Jane walk down the aisle hand in hand. You can breathe—everyone made it through the ceremony in one piece. Now, who's ready to party?

❧ To go to the reception, go to page 263.

Helena L. Paige

❧ It's time for the wedding reception

AS IF THE BRIDESMAID dress from hell wasn't punishment enough, you've been placed at the table with Tom's uncle Charlie, who is not only a lecher and a bore, but appeared to be three sheets to the wind during the wedding itself. Cee Cee is obviously getting her revenge on you for defrocking the priest. Well played, Cee Cee, well played.

The dressmaker managed to let out the seams of your dress a little so you could almost get the zipper all the way closed. But there was nothing she could do about the fabric, which you can now confirm does indeed match the tablecloths and napkins. And your boobs are so squashed by the bodice of the dress, they risk overflowing every time you breathe out. Uncle Charlie has barely been able to take his eyes off them, and the only thing stopping you from hitting him over the head with an empty champagne bottle is the fact that you don't want to cause a scene and ruin Jane's day (after your shenanigans with the priest, you've done quite enough already). Fortunately he looks like he's on the verge of passing out.

Even though you can't see her doing it, you're sure Aunt Lauren is having an illicit cigarette at the table next to yours—how else do you explain the odd plume of smoke that drifts past your nose? You also notice that she has her eye on Mikey—and on Tom's dad.

Still, in spite of your dress matching the décor, Uncle Charlie's leers, and the secondhand smoke, the wedding is going beautifully so far. There have been photographs, there have been toasts, there have been speeches, and there has been one damn hot DJ.

"Cute dress!"

You swivel in your seat as Mikey crouches down next to you, getting a good look down your very exposed cleavage. All you can think is monkey penis, monkey penis, monkey penis. You'll never be able to look at this doctor, clearly without borders, the same way ever again.

"Am I imagining things, or does it match the tablecloths? And the napkins?" he asks.

"Yes, you're imagining things!" you snap.

"Well, you make it look good. Want to dance?"

You'd like a chance to check out the DJ from closer quarters, so you agree—which you regret as soon as you hit the packed dance floor. Mikey gyrates in front of you, dancing exactly like a man with a monkey penis.

You try to ignore him and focus on the DJ. He's funky, but not in a pretentious-hipster way. And he plays good music, too—you love this track. There's been none of that awful wedding crap: no "Macarena," "Chicken Dance," or "Gangnam Style" yet, for which you are deeply grateful. Best of all, he hasn't played "Every Breath You Take," which always makes you think of stalkers. He looks up from his decks, a set of headphones clutched between his ear and shoulder, and catches your eye. He smiles and raises his hand, and you smile back, wishing that you weren't stuffed into this dreadful dress.

You notice that Tom's dad is trying to attract your attention, but Aunt Lauren has him firmly in her grasp.

The DJ points at Mikey, spinning like a lunatic next to you, and nods in mock approval. Mikey's so lost in his moves, he hasn't noticed you drifting away from him. You mime shooting yourself in the head. The DJ throws his head back and laughs, and you instantly want to lick his neck, where one of the tattoos snakes up out of the neckline of his shirt.

You and Mikey dance the next track in a big circle together with Domino and the Domino-ettes. Jane and Tom join you, and so do Lisa, Bruno, and Cat. You've been avoiding Bruno since the whole footsie thing—you've had bigger problems to deal with. But he keeps looking at you, and you're not going to be able to dodge him forever. There are things you need to discuss. Like why he was confessing his feelings for you on the balcony last night, and why he was playing footsie with you with his girlfriend sitting right next to him. Definitely not cool, even if you had seen Cat making out with Lisa.

You're also going to have to talk to Lisa. If there's

something going on between the two of them, she and Cat owe it to Bruno to be straight with him. And then there's the matter of Tom's dad, the pilot you were supposed to spend one night with and never see again. And yet right now, he's gazing at you across a room crowded with people you both know. Everything has managed to get very complicated in a very short space of time.

A new song starts, a slow number. You give the DJ an exasperated look and he shrugs apologetically. Mikey's about to pull you into an embrace when a bejeweled hand attached to a long arm covered in leopard print taps him on his shoulder. It's Aunt Lauren—who is either acting as your savior or has decided she's in the mood for a younger man. She gives Mikey her most lascivious grin.

"Care to dance?" she asks, her voice throaty.

"Actually I was just going to . . ." Mikey starts, indicating you.

"It's okay, I was going to sit this one out anyway," you say.

Uncle Charlie has finally passed out, his body slumped across your chair. You sit down at the neighboring table, and as you glance around the romantically lit room, it dawns on you that you're the only person not dancing. Every single guest is up and slow dancing with a partner. The pilot—Jack—is dancing with Jane's mom, Mikey is trapped in Aunt Lauren's grip, Bruno is wrangling toddlers in the middle of the dance floor, and where the hell is Lisa? What good is it going to a wedding with a friend if she keeps abandoning you?

"Ahem, excuse me."

That had better not be dirty Uncle Charlie, back from the dead.

"I was hoping you'd dance with me?" It's the hot DJ. He's holding out his hand, and you surreptitiously wipe your palm on your napkin dress, then allow him to lead you onto the dance floor.

"I really hope this isn't a pity dance because I was the only person not dancing," you say, enjoying the sensation of leaning against his long, lean body.

"Are you crazy? I had to bribe Jane's aunt to get the best man away from you."

You laugh, deciding not to ask what she wanted in return for the favor, and your stomach fizzes as if you've just swallowed sherbet.

"In fact, I've been wondering all afternoon if it would be appropriate to abandon my decks and ask you to dance. But I didn't want to piss off the bride."

"Don't worry, I've filled her pissed-off quota for the weekend, so you should be safe."

He spins you around. "That's a really hot dress, by the way," he says.

"Now I know you're lying."

"I've seen worse."

"No, you haven't!"

"You're right, I haven't. It's what a dress would look like if Lady Gaga and Laura Ashley got into a fight in a fabric shop. But I was trying to be polite."

He twirls you around again, and you feel like you're dancing on air.

a girl walks into a wedding

267

"I'd better get back to the decks. Thanks for the dance. I hope you'll save me another?" he says, returning you smoothly to your table.

"I guess that depends what you play."

You hear tapping on the microphone.

It's Mikey. "And now, the moment you've all been waiting for! It's time for Jane to throw her bouquet. Can we have all the single ladies on the dance floor?" he says.

Monkey penis, monkey penis, monkey penis, you think as you search the room for Lisa. You are not doing this without her. Thank goodness—she's clacking her way toward you, mischief all over her face. You and Lisa hover with the other women. Some feign lack of interest, others limber up, getting ready to make their big catch of the day. You and Lisa jostle each other, pretending this is important. Lisa lifts her heel behind her, holds it, and stretches like an Olympic athlete. You both laugh. Jane stands on a chair on the far side of the dance floor, and the DJ plays a quick drumroll. As it reaches its crescendo, Jane releases the bouquet, and it flies in slow motion through the air.

Helena S. Paige

❧ If you catch the bouquet, go to page 269.

❧ If you don't catch the bouquet, go to page 291.

 ❧ You catch the bouquet

YOU KNOW THE LEGEND—WHOEVER catches the bouquet will be the next to get married, or the next to get laid. You wouldn't mind testing out the latter theory, especially if the hot DJ is on the menu.

Lisa is standing next to you, her arms crossed over her chest. You cross your arms, too, in solidarity.

The bouquet travels as if in slow motion, and dips about four rows in front of you. A woman jumps into the air and swipes the tumbling stems with the tips of her fingers. The bouquet bounces off her fingers and carries on through the air straight toward you. It all happens so quickly, you don't have a chance to move, and the stalk of the bouquet lodges hard between your arms and your chest.

You hear applause as everyone steps away from you, opening up a circle of space around you. You caught it. You accidentally caught the damn bouquet!

"Now calling all the single men," Mikey says, dumping the microphone and making a dash for the dance floor, almost knocking the now roused Uncle Charlie off his feet as they both jostle for a good spot.

Clutching the bouquet, you step to the edge of the dance floor to watch. Jane stands on a chair, the lights are lowered, and the DJ puts on a classic bump-and-grind track. The guys whoop as Tom lifts Jane's skirt and rolls the garter down from the top of her thigh. Jane leans on Tom's shoulders for balance as he slips it off over her foot. Then he helps her down, kisses her, and takes his place on the chair, his back to the assembled guests. He waits a couple of beats, and then, as the crowd breaks into a slow clap, he flicks the garter into the waiting sea of bachelors.

❧ If Tom's dad catches the garter, go to page 271.

❧ If the DJ catches the garter, go to page 279.

❧ If Mikey catches the garter, go to page 286.

Helena L. Paige

Tom's dad catches the garter

YOU WATCH THE GARTER soar through the air, and as if on a preordained course, it lands neatly in the pilot's hands. It doesn't even look as if he reached for it.

"You have got to be kidding me!" you say to Lisa.

"It does have a certain pleasing symmetry to it," Lisa says. "Finish the weekend the way you started it."

"Hello, stranger," Tom's dad whispers in your ear as he walks you onto the dance floor and takes you in his arms for the obligatory bouquet-and-garter-catchers and bride-and-groom slow dance.

"Hello back," you whisper. "We're going to have to stop meeting like this."

"Do we?" he says. "I rather like meeting like this."

"I can't believe you're Tom's dad!"

"Don't you think it's time you started calling me Jack?" His strong fingers splay against your lower back as he guides you effortlessly around the dance floor. "Besides, we have a lot of catching up to do."

You're not sure what to say—you'd never planned on seeing this guy again, he's ruining your one-night stand.

"I was wondering how you're getting back to town after the wedding?" Jack asks, pressing his thumb gently into the center of your palm.

"Lisa and I were going to take the train." You slide your free hand from his shoulder to his chest, and he tugs you even closer.

"That's a pity. I was hoping I could give you a lift. I'm traveling by private jet," he says, dropping it in effortlessly.

"Jet?" you say.

"Call it a pilot perk. I have to deliver a plane to one of my billionaire clients tomorrow."

"Count me in!"

"Lisa won't mind?"

"I think she'll understand. What time is takeoff?"

"I'm ready whenever you are," he says, and you can feel the heat of his hand burning into the base of your spine.

"Okay, but you're going to have to let me change out of this awful dress before we leave. I couldn't possibly wear it on a jet."

"If you want. Or . . ."

"Or?" you ask.

"Or we could get on the plane, and then I could help you take it off," he murmurs.

Screw one-night stands, you're going in for a two-night stand.

"OKAY, I HAVE GOOD news and I have bad news," says Jack. "The bad news is that we can't take off for another two hours because of fog at our destination."

"And the good news?" You can't believe this is really happening—you're in a private jet, just you and Jack. Okay, so the plane is still on the ground, but you weren't going to refuse his offer of a tour of his cockpit.

"The good news is that we can't take off for another two hours. But you can help me with preflight checks, if you like."

"Just tell me what to do. Copilot at your service," you say, saluting him.

"Excellent. Well, it's simple. You just have to do absolutely everything the captain tells you to do from now on."

"Everything?"

"To the letter. Lives depend on it," he says.

"So what do prechecks entail?" you ask.

"Well, first I need to check that you get out of that dress. It's a fire hazard."

"Aye aye, Captain!" you say, turning in the narrow confines of the cockpit so he can pull the zipper down, the way you've seen it done in movies. He obliges, but the zipper sticks and he can't get it to budge.

You both laugh.

a girl walks into a wedding

"I think we need more room," he says. He opens the cockpit door and you enter the cabin, which is small but luxurious. There's a bar area made of walnut, four large, wide leather seats, and a large-screen TV.

"Now where did we leave off?" You can feel his fingers on your back as he tugs at the stubborn zipper.

"Just tear the damn thing," you say.

You hear the rip of fabric, then Jack slips the dress off your shoulders and it drops to the floor. He turns you to face him, and you aren't wearing a bra under the dress, so you're in nothing but panties and heels. He looks at you for a long moment, whispers, "Wow," and brings his mouth down onto yours.

Kissing him is familiar, yet entirely new at the same time. You had forgotten how well your mouths fit together. But this time he's clean-shaven, so there's none of that stubbly texture you remember from before. He slips his fingers down your back, and you pull his shirt out of his trousers so you can run your fingertips up under it and against his bare chest.

"I think we might be about to experience some turbulence," he says.

"Do I need to assume the position, Captain?" you say, your voice gruff with desire.

"You might need to hold on tight and prepare for a bumpy landing." He loosens his tie and then pulls his shirt off over his head, not bothering with the buttons, some of which pop off and ping across the cabin.

You run your mouth down his chest, grazing one of

his nipples with your teeth. Then you undo his buckle and unbutton his trousers, which slip to the ground. He steps out of them and pulls off his shoes and socks. You release his cock, already hard and pulsing, from his boxers, and as you clasp it in your palm, you feel the now familiar bend of it, how it curves to the left.

"You'll be pleased to hear that I'm a little better prepared this time," he says. As he steps away to fiddle in the pocket of his discarded jacket, you climb into one of the luxurious leather seats. The feel of the soft leather on your skin is sensational, and your body beats with desire as you wait for him.

He returns from across the cabin with a bottle of champagne in one hand, a glass in the other, and the plastic sleeve of a condom clamped between his teeth.

"Champagne?" he mumbles through the condom, passing you the glass. He pops the bottle and stands in front of you in nothing but his boxer shorts. The champagne fizzes and overflows from your glass, some of it spilling onto your chest.

"Wait, don't move—let me get that." He puts the bottle and condom on a small stand and crouches between your legs, then slowly licks the drops of champagne off your chest. You lie back and groan in delight as his hot tongue laps first at one nipple and then the other one, and then between your breasts.

"Sorry to be so clumsy. Out of practice," he says, as he licks the last splashes off your chest.

"Wait, I think you missed a spot."

a girl walks into a wedding

"Where?"

"Here," you say, gesturing to a point just below your breast, on your rib cage.

"Oh? How careless of me, let me fix that right away," he says, making a big show of leaning forward and lapping at the spot you identified. "How's that?" he asks.

"Great, but you missed another one over here," you say, pointing at your nipple, which is hard and ridged.

He grins and lowers his head again, this time not licking, but taking the entire nipple in his mouth, supporting your breast with one hand, while running his other hand over your other breast, rolling the nipple between his fingers.

"And here," you whisper, when he eventually lifts his head. And you point to your panties.

"Oh my goodness, you're soaked," he says hoarsely, dropping his mouth between your legs. "I didn't realize I'd spilled so much. I'd better do something about that."

You put both hands on his head as he sucks at you hard through your panties, and you feel yourself gushing. Then you lift your hips as he pulls them off and sinks his head down into your pussy, first nipping very gently, then taking your lips into his mouth and sucking them. You writhe in the chair, but you don't want to come just yet, so after a few minutes of bliss, you tug his head away, whispering that you need him to stop.

Jack gets to his feet and reaches for your hand, pulling you up and enveloping you in his arms again. As you kiss, you can feel that beautiful hard, bent cock pressing against you. You reach for the condom beside the forgotten champagne, get it out of its package, and then roll it down over his cock, using one hand over the other.

He spins you around and you can feel his body pressed against your back as he works his teeth and tongue against your neck, his hands running down your chest, exploring your breasts and nipples. Then he takes one hand lower, running it down your stomach and over your mound, sliding a couple of fingers up and down your slit before slipping a finger inside your pussy. You moan, and he pushes another finger inside you, slowly rocking them in and out, his palm pressing down on your mound, teasing your clit, never touching it directly.

"Fuck me," you whisper, and make as if to turn around.

"Wait," he says. "Stay like that, trust me."

You lean forward a little, resting your arms on the back of the leather seat for balance, as you part your legs. You feel every inch of his hard bent cock rubbing against you before he guides it inside you from behind. You adjust to the size and shape of him as he pushes slowly into you, both hands on your hips for leverage. You groan at his first thrust, a different sensation now that he's inside of you, something new. You can feel the head of his cock brushing your G-spot. It must be the bend that makes him able to reach that elusive spot, causing intense pleasure to radiate through your body with every movement of his cock.

You can't help crying out, and this makes him

plunge into you even more frantically. You push backward at him in turn, until the pleasure is so intense and the fucking so furious, you can barely stand it.

Then he steps back, slipping out of you, and you growl in frustration. He moves around you to sit on the leather recliner and pulls you back down onto him, astride his lap, your back against his chest.

You're so wet, he slips back inside you effortlessly. Now you're the one riding him, clutching his thighs for leverage, controlling how hard he hits your G-spot with every thrust going deeper and harder than the one before.

As you're about to go over the edge, you clamp down on his cock in a series of quick pulses and come with a cry, your pussy contracting and releasing again and again. And he shudders and shouts out as he comes inside you.

You lean back against his chest, and feel the world around you giving way as Jack pulls the lever of the chair to recline it all the way back, and snags a blanket out of nowhere. You settle alongside him, relishing the sense of honey spreading through your veins.

"I hope you enjoyed the flight," he whispers in your ear as he tucks a strand of your hair behind it. "And that you'll choose this airline again." He looks down at his already stiffening cock. "I estimate takeoff will commence in about fifteen minutes."

"Roger that, Captain," you say with a satisfied smile.

The End

Helena S. Paige

❧ The DJ catches the garter

 TOM CLEARLY DOESN'T KNOW his own strength. He launches the garter over his shoulder, and it flies right over the grasping fingertips of the jostling bachelors and lands in the middle of a surprised DJ Salinger's decks.

He scoops it up and dangles it from a finger. Someone starts clapping, and everyone else follows suit.

As the cake-cutting begins, the DJ joins you at your table.

"You've clearly been to more weddings than me—what does this mean?" you ask, pointing at his garter, then at your bouquet.

"It means that you and I have to get married," he says.

"Ha, ha. Surely not!"

"I think if you check the literature, you'll find that's the truth."

Coming over all tongue-tied, you buy time by reaching for your glass of red wine and taking a sip. That's odd—there's something in your mouth. You swill it around, trying to identify it while keeping a sophisticated expression on your face.

"Mommy!" wails Tokyo or Timbuktu or Toledo. "I can't find Yodabell's bow tie!"

Oh no. It can't be. You test the object gently with your tongue. It certainly feels like it could be the missing rodent accessory.

You reflexively spit it out in a projectile stream of red wine, which hits the DJ squarely in the chest and spatters down the front of his white shirt.

"What the hell?" he cries, jumping back.

You don't think you've ever felt this mortified. But you're hugely relieved to spot a sodden piece of paper clinging to his stained shirt. Thankfully the foreign object was only the detritus from a party popper. "I'm so sorry," you say to him. "But I thought I was about to swallow a rat's bow tie."

He looks at you for the longest minute as if you're completely insane, and then you both burst out laughing.

"Oh god, it's going to take a lifetime to explain, and I'm about to die of embarrassment," you say, when you manage to get yourself under control. "Can we take my total humiliation as a given and go and soak your shirt? I'll feel awful if you never manage to get that stain out."

* * *

"I REALLY AM SORRY!" you say, as you stand at the double sink in your bathroom, scrubbing at the stubborn stain with a bar of hotel soap.

"Please don't apologize. I'm very impressed. Normally I'm the one trying to come up with nifty ideas of how to get a girl back to my room with her shirt off, not the other way around."

"I don't normally invite half-naked men into my room, but there are extenuating circumstances in this case."

You run water to soak the shirt and move to the second sink. Even though Yodabell the rat's wedding finery was nowhere near your mouth, you still feel a bit squeamish. As you brush your teeth, you check the DJ out in the mirror as he leans casually against the shower door. Now that his shirt is off, you can admire not only the well-defined muscles on his arms, but the black-inked tattoos that scroll around them.

"So do you have a name, Mr. DJ?" you ask as you pat your mouth with a towel.

"It's JD," he says.

"For real?"

He nods.

"JD the DJ?"

"What about you?" he asks. "I'm going to need to know who to send the cleaning bill to."

You tell him your name and then brush your teeth for a second time. As you finish, JD moves beside you at the sink, looking at your reflection in the mirror, his arm brushing yours. It's an oddly intimate moment, and it's not just the mirror that's steaming up a little.

"Better?" he asks.

"I think so," you say, running your tongue over your now freshly gleaming teeth.

"Perhaps I could offer a second opinion?" he offers.

Your cheeks go flame-hot, and your heart starts to thump as he turns you to face him and kisses you gently on the mouth. You feel his tongue run across your lips and you part them a little. The heat of his tongue is cooled by the freshness of the toothpaste on yours.

You loop your arms around him, and when the kiss comes to an end, he snakes his arms around your waist, too, linking you closely.

"Hmmm, minty fresh." He lowers his arms even farther and lifts you onto the space between the two sinks. Something falls to the floor and breaks, but it doesn't matter, because he's kissing you again, and this time you get to run your hands up his naked arms and over his chest, and then the little pebbles of his nipples.

His hands roam over your neck and shoulders, and one caresses your breast over the fabric of your dress, which is so stiff, you can't feel his fingers, to your frustration. You lean back against the mirror, your hand slips, and you swear as you bash your funny bone against the tap.

"Look," JD says, "I know all the cool kids are getting off in bathrooms, but would you mind if we went old-school and moved this party into the bedroom?"

"I thought you'd never ask—my comb is poking me in the ass, and not in a good way."

You stand beside the bed, kissing again, slowly swinging your pelvis from side to side against him. He tries to undo some of the buttons on your dress, but they won't budge. You forgot that in desperation, you used generous amounts of safety pins earlier so that the bodice wouldn't pop open every time you took a breath.

JD gives up on the front of your dress and reaches behind you for the zipper, but finds that stuck, too. It's as if you're glued to this stupid dress!

JD laughs and collapses back onto the bed. You're desperate to have his hands all over you, but the dress is having none of it.

"Wait a minute," you say, diving into your suitcase and digging around. "Cut me out of this fucking thing, I'm begging you!" you say, fishing out a pair of emergency scissors and handing them to him.

"Are you sure?" he asks.

"Absolutely!" You lie down on the bed and he kneels alongside you, holding the scissors poised at your hem.

"Really sure?" he asks again.

"Hell yeah!"

You feel his hand on your ankle as he tugs your legs slightly apart, then slowly works the scissors from the hem up your leg, running his hand behind the blade. All you can hear is both of you breathing heavily and the schick, schick of the scissors as they eat through the heavy fabric, the blade cool against your skin as it climbs your leg.

He straddles your leg as he moves higher and higher, the scissors followed by his fingers, followed by his tongue. As he cuts, your dress falls to each side in piles. He slows as he reaches the top of your leg, and nuzzles your inner thigh with his nose, teeth, and lips. Then at last he strokes you with his fingers and you groan and open your legs a little more, so he has access to the part of you that you really want him to touch now.

He lifts the fabric of your underwear, stretching it upward, and then you feel the cold metal of the scissors against your mound as he cuts through your pants and the dress at the same time, slicing up over your pubic bone until your panties are just a shredded memory. And then finally he cuts up the bodice alongside the buttons, and you sit up to help him release the sleeves from your arms, so that you're completely naked, finally rid of the weight of the fabric, so that now it's just skin against skin.

You strip his trousers off in seconds, freeing his cock into one eager hand and covering his balls with your other one, massaging them gently. He pushes his knee between your legs and you can feel your wet pussy pressing against his thigh, the sense of friction so good, you writhe against him.

You tell him that you'll be right back and dash to the bathroom to retrieve a condom from your toiletry bag, smiling at the stained shirt soaking in the basin, before heading back to him.

You pause for a second to take in the sight of him,

his tattoos snaking down his arms and onto his chest, his dusky erection rearing up. Then you kneel over him, fit the condom over the head of his cock, and roll on the rest of it with your mouth. Mmm, what his cock lacks in length, it makes up for in girth.

He lays you on the bed and lowers himself between your legs. You feel his cock nudging against the opening of your pussy, then sinking into you, hot and powerful. It's such a relief to be filled up by him that you bite down on his shoulder as he thrusts into you, pulling himself almost all the way out of you on each stroke, driving you wild to be filled up once more.

Then you reach down between your heaving bodies, circle your thumb and forefinger around the base of his cock, and squeeze to create even more pressure as he pounds into you. You lock your legs around him tightly, crossing your ankles and angling your hips so that he penetrates you even deeper, and then you can't think about anything anymore. And you start coming, your pussy clutching his cock repeatedly as he keeps thrusting, rotating your hips as you push up to meet him, until you feel him shuddering against you, every muscle stiffening for a split second before the final release.

You cover your naked, spent bodies with a blanket from the end of the bed and lie tracing the Gothic patterns on his arm.

"Looks like catching the garter has fringe benefits," he whispers in your ear as you drift off into a delicious doze.

a girl walks into a wedding

The End

285

❧ Mikey catches the garter

JUST AS THE GARTER is about to land squarely in Bruno's hands, Mikey swoops down and grabs it. Saving lives, evading the tax man and extreme climbing have clearly gifted him with ninja reflexes. Bruno's face drops when he realizes it's been snatched from right under his nose, and you feel a little sorry for him, but relieved at the same time. You've been avoiding him ever since the whole footsie episode at the rehearsal dinner last night, and traditionally, whoever catches the bouquet has to slow dance with whoever catches the garter. So while you're not all that pleased it's monkey-boy, at least you can avoid Bruno for a little longer.

You've done a U-turn about him this weekend—he's grown into such a nice guy, sweet, funny, kind, and even cute—but he's here with Cat, and it really bothers you that he's been coming on to you.

And then there's the whole thing between Cat and Lisa. You're worried that if you end up talking to Bruno, you're going to have to tell him what's been going on behind his back all weekend. No, it's definitely easier if you simply avoid him. And speaking of avoiding people . . . Mikey strides purposefully toward you, a smug expression on his face.

"Hey, beautiful," he smarms, dangling the garter from the end of his finger. "Look what I got."

The lights over the dance floor go low and something suitably slow and romantic starts to play.

"May I have this dance?" he asks.

"I don't think so," you say curtly. What kind of bastard best man makes a pass at the bride two nights before her wedding?

He's undeterred. "It's okay, I understand—you're scared you won't be able to keep your hands off me."

"Yes, that's it," you say, your voice deadpan. Then, over Mikey's shoulder, you spot Bruno walking toward you, a man on a mission. "I've changed my mind," you say, launching into Mikey's arms and shoving him onto the dance floor.

"Easy, tiger. I knew you couldn't resist the Mikey-nator!" he says, wrapping his octopus arms around you. Within seconds you feel one of his hands drop onto your bottom. You reach behind and lift it off, only to feel it clamping back on immediately.

The second the song comes to an end, you break away from Mikey and turn to leave the dance floor, only to find your way blocked by a determined-looking Bruno. Before he can speak, you collar Mikey once again. "Another one!" you yell at him.

Mikey grins manically and pulls you much too close as the dance floor fills up around you once again. As he sweeps you around, you feel a tap on your shoulder. You turn, hoping it's not Bruno. Thankfully, it's Cat.

"Mind if I cut in?" she asks.

"Of course not." You step away, a little confused. "He's all yours."

"No shoving, ladies, I have more than enough love to go around." Mikey gleefully holds his arms open to you both.

"Not him, you," Cat says, looking you in the eye.

You swallow, your mouth instantly dry. What could she possibly want with you? You feel incredibly awkward about seeing her with Lisa. And what if she's noticed the looks Bruno has been casting your way?

Before you know what's happening, you're dancing with Cat. She's taller than you, and she leads gracefully, guiding you around the dance floor to the slow track pumping through the speakers. Dancing with another woman feels odd, especially after dancing with monkey-boy. Her hands feel disconcertingly small.

"What the hell do you think you're doing?" Cat hisses at you once you're swaying around the floor.

"Nothing! Nothing's happened, I swear!"

"Well, I don't know why not, he's a phenomenal guy," Cat says.

"Wait—who are we talking about?"

"Bruno, of course. Can't you see how crazy he is about you?"

"But aren't you and he . . ."

Cat starts to laugh. "Bruno and me, a couple? We've been friends for years, and anyway, I don't bat for that team. I just came with him to get his mother off his back about him still being single. She can be a bit of a pain. But tell you what, if I bent that way, Bruno would be my number one choice."

"You mean you're not into guys?"

"Nope."

"Oh, thank god! That explains you and Lisa. I saw you in the laundry room the other night."

"Oh, you did, did you?" She chuckles. "Well, that was tame. Just be grateful you didn't see us on the pool table, in the summerhouse, or in the sauna."

"All this time, I thought you and Bruno were together—that's why I've been avoiding him."

"I noticed!" Cat says, twirling you around, and as she does, you see Bruno off to one side watching you, his face a picture of angst. Your heart softens—you've been a little harsh on the poor guy.

"I know it's not really my business, but would you do me a favor and just give him a chance? He's totally mad about you, and you could do far worse." Cat nods over at Mikey, who's standing on the edge of the dance floor watching you and Cat lasciviously and making lewd gestures.

"I think I can do that," you say, a slow smile of antici-pation starting to break out.

Cat steps away from you and you find yourself standing stock-still and partnerless in the center of the dance floor. But you're not alone for long. Holding your eyes, Bruno slowly walks toward you and stretches out his hand. You feel a slight tingle as your palms touch, and then he draws you to him.

"Finally," he breathes in your ear.

"Finally," you echo, your voice cracking.

You rest your cheek against his, inhaling his scent, the warmth of his body pressing against yours. Could it be that the very thing you've been longing for has been right under your nose all along?

Then he kisses you, and you know that yes, this was meant to be.

The End

Helena L. Paige

❧ You don't catch the bouquet

THE GIRLS JOSTLE IN a tight bunch as the bouquet flies through the air. It takes you only a second to realize that it's heading straight for Lisa. She has a look of terror on her face, as if she's about to catch a hand grenade rather than a bunch of white daisies, roses, and baby's breath laced in satin ribbons.

Lisa shoots you a pleading look, and without a second thought, you spring into action. You shove her out of the way and step forward to deflect the bouquet—and from there everything happens in slow motion.

You realize that it must look like you were pushing Lisa out of the way so you could catch the bouquet yourself. But you don't have time to contemplate how bad that must make you look, because you bash heads with another woman, who's launching her body through the air like an NBA basketball player.

The pain of the collision is instant and excruciating. Who knew the human head was made of concrete?

YOU BLINK, OPENING YOUR eyes slowly. You have the worst headache ever. It starts at the base of your skull and embraces your entire head.

You look up and see swathes of muslin above you—you're lying on a four-poster bed. The disastrous bouquet toss comes flooding back to you. Then you see the pilot's face swim into view above yours. Tom's dad. Jack.

"What happened?" you whisper.

"You took a tumble in the battle for the bride's bouquet and banged your head. You're in the wedding suite. Everyone is downstairs seeing the bride and groom off. I said I'd keep an eye on you."

"Am I okay?" you ask, your voice husky.

"Yes, the hotel called a doctor to take a look at you, and she says you'll be fine—you're just very mildly concussed. No heavy lifting or competitive bouquet catching for a little while."

It's coming back to you now—you remember a very crisp woman shining a penlight in your eyes and taking your pulse.

Jack helps you sit up and stacks some pillows behind your back, then hands you a glass of water. You whimper a little, feeling sorry for yourself. What a way to end the wedding!

"Where does it hurt?" Jack asks, concern creasing his brow.

"Over here," you say, pointing at your forehead.

Jack leans over you and presses his mouth gently on the spot you indicated.

"And over here," you say, touching your eye.

Jack leans in again, and kisses you delicately on your eyelid.

"And over here," you say, beginning to smile as you touch your mouth.

Jack smiles, too, then leans in one more time, kissing you on the lips as carefully as if you were made of porcelain. He manages to be both passionate and gentle, and you close your eyes and surrender to his kiss, enjoying the sensation of his tongue in your mouth, and his arms cradling you. You see stars exploding behind your eyes, and this time it's nothing to do with a blow to the head.

The End

a girl walks into a wedding

🕭 You choose the justice of the peace

YOU STAND AT THE back of the church while you wait for Jane to arrive, and look down the aisle, appraising the justice of the peace. You're sure Jane will love her. She's just right for the job—calm in a neat navy-blue suit, with a warm smile.

Surely after everything that's happened, nothing more can go wrong—or can it?

🕭 If the wedding ends happily ever after, go to page 295.

🕭 If the wedding doesn't end happily ever after, go to page 299.

✎ The wedding ends happily ever after

IT'S BEEN THE MOST perfect wedding imaginable. Everything has gone without a hitch, and Cee Cee is practically purring with pride.

The guests all turned out in their best finery, with Aunt Lauren stealing the show. She even donned a hat, a hot-pink tiger-striped cartwheel adorned with what looked like a large lobster.

Jane was a vision as she floated down the aisle on her father's arm to the accompaniment of a string quartet and a blonde soprano in purple taffeta performing Bach's "Jesu, Joy of Man's Desiring." Tom almost choked with emotion as she joined him at the altar, the sunlight shining through the stained glass windows, casting jeweled splashes on her exquisite vintage dress.

Even the little flower girls behaved beautifully, solemnly carrying their baskets of organic rose petals and earning aahs from the assembled guests.

The justice of the peace was absolutely the right choice, with her wise words and gentle manner.

You watched with a lump in your throat as your best friend's face bloomed into radiance as she joined Tom. Once they were pronounced husband and wife, the choir burst into the "Hallelujah Chorus," echoing your own emotions.

As the newlyweds and the elegantly dressed guests left the church, hundreds of white butterflies were released. It was Cee Cee's finest hour, as they drifted and fluttered up into the clear blue sky, a symbol of hope and transformation.

And miracle of miracles, the dressmaker seemed to have let out an extra seam—even though your dress is still tight, at least it's not a disgrace.

The reception went off without a hitch, and the six-tiered mocha hazelnut cake was the best wedding cake you'd ever tasted. And to wind up her day of triumph, Cee Cee caught the bride's bouquet.

Now you're standing in the driveway, still smiling at the memory of the warm, funny speeches (even Mikey's best-man speech was just the right mix of humor and affection), waving off Tom and Jane, who decided to go straight off on their honeymoon rather than spend a night in the bridal suite. The lowering sun catches the ripples of the lake, painting it in streaks of gold, and as the happy couple drives away in a silver vintage Roller, the swans take off, trumpeting in salute.

You sigh wistfully. Your best friend just got married! Then you sense someone by your side. It's Bruno, and you realize with a slight shock, as the late sun gilds his features, that up until now you've entirely missed how good-looking he really is. He smiles at you, his eyes dark and kind, and takes your hand, his fingers caressing yours. "What do you say you and I try out our own happily ever after?" he asks.

You're about to answer when Mikey sidles up to you. "How about a drink to toast the happy couple?"

You glance at Bruno. "Why not?" he says.

THE FIRST THING THAT hits you is that it's early morning. The second thing that hits you is that you appear to be in the bridal suite. The third thing that hits you is that there are bodies scattered everywhere. Half-naked bodies.

You sit up and peer around the room through bleary eyes. Aunt Lauren and Cee Cee are half-hidden under the bed, both dead to the world, both clutching empty bottles of Moët.

Lisa, Tom's dad, and Cat are lying in each other's arms on the carpet next to the open, empty minibar. The receptionist and the DJ—both wearing bridesmaids' dresses—are snoring on the balcony, their hands linked.

And . . . is that Bruno curled around the TV cabinet? It is. And there's something protruding from his bottom. Something that looks suspiciously like a G.I. Joe figure wearing scuba gear.

You swing your legs off the bed and somehow

manage to get your balance. Whoa. You peer inside the bathroom and see a man wearing nothing but a motorcycle helmet lying in the bathtub. You can't be certain, but it looks like it might be Mikey.

You wrap yourself in a sheet and stagger into the hallway. It's littered with empty champagne bottles and streamers, and the half-eaten wedding cake is perched on top of a cleaning cart, Yodabell the rat happily tucking into it.

Slowly the night's events start to come back to you. After you all waved off Jane and Tom, Mikey brought out a couple of bottles of fiery liquor from one of his jaunts in Africa, you all had a shot, and things went downhill from there. There was dancing (at one point, Cee Cee got up on the bridal table to show off her moves), then someone suggested you all do a conga line into the bridal suite. And then . . .

Wow. Did you really . . . ? And how could . . . ? And is that even anatomically possible?

You let yourself into your room and pad toward the shower, smiling to yourself.

What a night.

What a wedding.

Happy endings all around.

The End

IT FEELS LIKE YOU'VE been holding your breath from the second Jane walked down the aisle. Cee Cee has outdone herself and the church looks gorgeous. And Jane seems happy with your choice of wedding officiant—you haven't had a single death glare from either her or Cee Cee. After the disaster with Father Declan, you're desperate for this to go well.

"Do you, Tom, take Jane to be your lawfully wedded wife?" the justice of the peace intones in a beautiful low voice.

Tom holds both of Jane's hands in his. "I do," he says.

One down, one to go. You're almost home free.

"And Jane, do you take Tom to be your lawfully wedded husband?"

You're sure your heart stops beating—if Jane's cold-feet issues resurface, this could all go horribly wrong in a split second.

"I . . . I . . ." Jane says, tears brimming in her eyes.

Adrenaline surges through your body.

"I do," she says at last. Oh, thank god. As the justice of the peace utters the timeless phrase "You may kiss the bride," you finally allow yourself to exhale. Despite some hairy moments, it looks like everything has worked out okay after all.

But you can't quite untie the knot in your stomach yet—there's still the reception to get through.

After a million photographs, the wedding party and guests file into the elaborately decorated function room for the reception. Champagne bottles pop. Waiters troop in bearing plates of hors d'oeuvres. After the main course—salmon and mustard leaf *en croute* with gratinated baby bok choy—it's time for the speeches. First Jane's father gives a tear-jerking speech, and then Tom stands up to toast the bridesmaids. You're not looking forward to Mikey's speech, but despite an off-color joke about a swan and a priest, it's not as crass as you were expecting. The wedding gods are clearly smiling down on you.

It's Jane's turn. You helped her choose a lovely poem by Emily Dickinson for the occasion, and you're looking forward to hearing her read it. You give her an encouraging smile. She really does look terribly nervous.

She clears her throat. "I need to begin by saying . . . that . . ."

Uh-oh. This isn't what you rehearsed.

"I kissed Mikey!" she blurts out.

There's a stunned silence. The blood drains from

Tom's face. Even more blood drains from Mikey's face. You dig your nails into your palms, hard enough to draw blood.

"Tom . . . it was an accident," Jane sobs. "It meant nothing! I swear—you have to believe me!"

"Tom! Buddy! I swear it really did mean nothing. I was bombed out of my mind," Mikey protests, his handsome face wild with panic.

Tom looks thoughtful for a second, then stands up and punches Mikey, who tumbles off his chair and stays down, clearly out for the count. You're impressed—who knew Tom had it in him?

Jane is sobbing in earnest now. "Tom, I'm so sorry, it was the biggest mistake of my life. I love you. I want to be with you, always. Please forgive me! You're my best friend—I had to tell you the truth!"

You wait, holding your breath, as Tom stands mute for several long seconds. Only the flick of Aunt Lauren's cigarette lighter breaks the silence in the room.

"Jane . . ." he starts. "I love you, too." He takes her in his arms. "I forgive you, I have to. Life without you isn't worth living." As they embrace, the room erupts, everyone cheering and clapping.

You collapse back in your seat and take a swig of champagne. Another bullet dodged. You notice Mikey is on his feet and edging toward the door, his hand massaging his chin. Good riddance, you think. It feels like everyone—with the exception of Mikey—will get their happily ever after, after all.

The DJ starts playing the song for the first dance,

and Tom and Jane glide into the center of the room, gazing into each other's eyes. It's a ballad, but for some reason there's a strange backing track. A droning sound—could it be feedback from the speakers? Then you hear bellowing and trumpeting along with the low hum. Heads are starting to swivel as others notice the unusual sound effects.

The next minute, an enormous bull crashes through French doors and charges across the room, snorting and bucking as if it's in Pamplona. On encountering the barriers presented by the dessert buffet, bar, and sound decks, it simply plows through them all.

Tom sweeps Jane out of harm's way, but everyone else is too shocked to move or scream. The noise of falling bottles, cutlery, and sound equipment goes on seemingly forever. The DJ rises from the wreckage unharmed but speechless, while the maddened animal tries to leap over the wedding cake, hampered by a tablecloth caught on its horns and roguishly draped over one eye. It makes a dramatic exit via another (closed) window, plunging through it in a shower of glass.

"Good god, Tom," says Bruno into the horrified hush that follows. "Dissatisfied patient of yours? Did you accidentally castrate the wrong beast?"

No one is hurt, although the cake is missing its top tier, but it's not over yet. Hot on the heels of the bull are swans—lots of swans. They strut into the reception room like storm troopers. For the first time, you realize what angry-looking birds they are, with their mean little button eyes and snaking necks.

Mikey, who's hovering at the door, clearly sees this as a chance to salvage his reputation. "Go on!" he says, flapping his hands at them. "Get out of here, you uppity ducks." The leader of the pack ("flock" seems too mild a word) sizes him up, then slashes wickedly at his kneecap. Mikey goes down—for the second time—with a howl. The swans hiss with agitation and look around for fresh blood. Everyone hastily withdraws behind their chairs, and Domino push their tots, who are squealing with glee rather than distress, under a table.

The swans waddle through the room, their heads darting from side to side like suspicious prison wardens. Several pause to crap lavishly on the carpet before they exit the same way as the bull.

Meanwhile, the ominous humming in the background has become a furious buzz, and the panic of the bull and the swans is explained when a swarm of bees rockets into the room. By now, people are scrambling for the doors. Fortunately, the bees aren't interested in human targets—in a great vibrating clump, they head for the cake and settle all over it. In seconds, its pristine white icing turns black as the bees gorge on the sweetness.

You and Domino scoop up the kids and the rat cage, and join the general stampede for the veranda. The shocked guests are milling around, buzzing almost as much as the bees. Apart from Mikey, who is hobbling away toward the parking lot, and a few unlucky folk who got random stings, everyone seems to be intact.

Jane points dramatically at Cee Cee, who is gibbering with horror. "This is all your fault!" she yells. "I wanted a chocolate wedding cake, but nooooooo. Too tacky, you said. All the best people are going for honey-and-nougat this season, you said. And now look!"

Aunt Lauren's spectacular hat rises cautiously from behind an overturned table. "Darlings," she purrs. "I'm not surprised the birds and the bees showed up. This is a wedding, after all."

The End

Helena L. Paige

☙ You've chosen the new age marriage officiant

As Jane enters the chapel, she turns and gives you the A-OK sign. You smile back nervously. The new age marriage officiant looks reassuringly ordinary from back here. You were expecting beads and feathers, but he's in his late forties, wearing dark trousers, and one of those floaty white shirts, no doubt spun on a sustainable wood loom. Jane isn't close enough to notice the ears pierced with large discs and the swirling tattoos creeping out from under both shirtsleeves, or the small fertility goddess hanging from a leather cord around his neck.

The organ starts to play, and first the Domino kids head down the aisle, then Cee Cee and you, holding your breath so that your breasts don't pop out of your dress, followed by Jane and her dad. This has to go smoothly, you think, it just has to.

Jane walks toward Tom, whose face is a picture of

happiness, and hope fills your heart. You really do believe they're going to be okay.

The ceremony gets underway, and you relax into it. The service is rather lovely in fact, with a few well-chosen poems. You might just get away with it.

"Do you, umm . . . what's your name again?" the officiant asks.

"Tom," Tom says.

"Ah yes, do you, Tom, take this woman . . ."

"Jane," Jane says.

". . . Jane, to be your lawful wedded wife?"

Cee Cee shoots you a dirty look, and you grin at her. Hey, nobody's perfect.

"You may kiss to seal your pact," the officiant says.

They kiss, and then just when you think it's all over and everything is going to be okay, the guru launches into one final speech.

"The coming together of two souls is a mystic thing. Two elements unable to live apart fuel the fire of passion together. Like oxygen to a flame." And then he pulls out a long stick and a bottle. There's a pungent smell of kerosene. Before anyone can stop him, he lights both ends of the stick, and they bloom into flames.

There's an appreciative hum of excitement from the wedding guests, and Jane and Tom step back from the flames, holding hands, watching in awe.

The officiant then proceeds to twirl the baton of fire between his fingers like a drum majorette, before holding one of the lit ends to his mouth and licking at the flame. Then he swallows the flame dramatically. The wedding guests applaud, oohing and aahing. As he spins the baton once more, relighting the extinguished side, which flares wildly, Cee Cee steps backward out of the way, pulling a face.

"See," you tell her, "this worked out fine! Bet nobody here has ever been to a wedding like this before!"

The guru holds the baton out in front of him, and first taking a mouthful of kerosene, he blows on it, causing a huge fireball to billow off the stick and fly down the aisle. But no detail has been left untended by Maid of Honor Extraordinaire, and there are a series of ribbons, in the same fabric as your dress, tied lovingly and elaborately onto the end of each pew. Within seconds, the fire-hungry fabric catches alight.

As panicked wedding guests scream and jostle to escape the pews—which are also starting to catch—the new age guru knocks over his bottle of kerosene, which floods out over the dry, ancient wooden floors. A finger of flame leaps to lap it up.

There's a stampede for the door. You grab Cee Cee, and Tom pulls Jane behind him.

Finally everyone is safely outside and accounted for, huddled in shock on the lawn, watching flames lick at the stained glass windows.

"Bet you *nobody* has ever been to a wedding like this before!" Cee Cee snarls in your ear.

Tom comes to your rescue. "Actually, Cee Cee, that's not necessarily a bad thing. Isn't this supposed to be a day to remember for the rest of your life? And who the hell is going to forget this?"

You smile at him gratefully.

"Forget this, we're going on our honeymoon!" Jane says, tugging Tom toward the waiting car, with JUST MARRIED daubed on the rear window and tin cans on pieces of string dangling from the bumper. Everyone cheers and waves as they speed away.

The sound of sirens grows louder and a fire engine roars down the driveway and screams to a halt in front of the burning chapel. Your eyes widen as a cluster of burly firefighters leap into action—you've never seen such a buff gang of rescuers. They must all do special firefighting exercises—even in their protective uniforms, it's muscle city everywhere you look.

They unravel huge hoses with practiced ease and begin training them on the windows.

"Stand back, ma'am!" says one Adonis to you. Is that a wink he's giving you? You smile blindingly at him, only to hear a voice in your ear: "He's married, with two small children."

It's Bruno. You gape at him. "How do you know?"

"Never seen him before in my life. I'm just using my superior brainpower to eliminate the brawny competition."

You start to giggle, and Bruno snakes an arm around your shoulders. You relax back against him, and it feels good—and then an undeniable frisson runs down your spine as he brushes his lips against your cheek.

As the firefighters wrestle with their pulsing hoses, moving back and forth in perfect synchronicity, timeless Aunt Lauren appears beside you in her fabulous

Helena S. Paige

leopard-print creation and gloriously clashing hat. "Darling, what fun. I've been to weddings with fireworks before, but nothing quite like this," she says, licking her lips as a particularly muscular fireman belts past her. "I just love a happy ending."

The End

Acknowledgments

WE'RE VERY GRATEFUL TO everyone who's shown faith in the Girl and her adventures. The list starts with our superhero agent, Oli Munson, and our fairy godmothers Jennifer Custer and Hélène Ferey, all of A.M. Heath & Company, who always seem to have good news for us. A big thank-you to every single publisher who's embraced the Girl, especially Manpreet Grewal and her team at Sphere (Little, Brown), Amanda Bergeron and crew at William Morrow (HarperCollins), and Jeremy Boraine and his colleagues (Jonathan Ball). We know there are editors, translators, designers, cover artists, typesetters, and many more people in twenty different countries working hard to make the Girl look good: thank you to all.

Thanks to Amber de Savary of the Old Swan and Minster Mill, and the other wedding planners and coordinators who showed us their romantic venues and shared their stories with us.

For advice, suggestions, and support both practical and moral, we are hugely grateful to: Candice, Carol, Charlie, Edyth, James, Kathy, Lauren, Liesl, Rosemary, Savannah, Steve, and Tom. May your condoms never break.

ABOUT THE AUTHORS

HELENA S. PAIGE is the pseudonym of authors Helen Moffett, Sarah Lotz, and Paige Nick. **HELEN MOFFETT** wears many hats: freelance writer, editor, researcher, poet, academic, and flamenco fan. **SARAH LOTZ** is a screenwriter and novelist with a fondness for fake names. She writes urban horror novels with author Louis Greenberg under the name S. L. Grey and a YA pulp fiction zombie series with her daughter, Savannah, under the pseudonym Lily Herne. **PAIGE NICK** is an author, award-winning advertising copywriter, and a weekly columnist for the *Sunday Times* (Johannesburg), covering everything from sex to dating and general lunacy.

BOOKS BY HELENA S. PAIGE

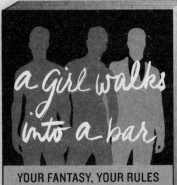

A GIRL WALKS INTO A BAR
Your Fantasy, Your Rules
Available in Paperback and eBook

How will your night out end? You make the rules. You're at one of the hottest bars in town, all dressed up for a fabulous girls' night out with your best friend, when she cancels. What do you do now? In this novel, YOU make the decisions. Will you do body shots with a rock star? Cozy up to the hot bartender? Follow a mysterious woman to a rather unusual exhibition? Investigate a suave millionaire's box of tricks? Take a joyride with a buff bodyguard? Or maybe what you want is closer to home than you realize. . . . So many options. . . . All you have to do is choose.

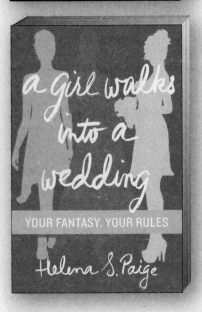

A GIRL WALKS INTO A WEDDING
Your Fantasy, Your Rules
Available in Paperback and eBook

YOU are invited to a wedding. As you try on what must be the ugliest bridesmaid dress you realize so much can go wrong with this event. Your best friend needs to know NOW if you are bringing a date. So what is a girl to do? Do you bring the sexy guy you have only gone on one date with, or do you brave it and go alone? In this novel, you make the decisions. Will your dream date turn out to be a dud? Will the best man find a way under your ugly dress? Will the bachelorette party end with a bang or a fizzle? Will the wedding even happen at all? All of these experiences are awaiting you at the beautiful country estate.